I0823259

THE RESERVATION

ALSO BY

REBECCA KAUFFMAN

I'll Come to You

Chorus

The House on Fripp Island

The Gunners

Another Place You've Never Been

THE RESERVATION

A Novel

REBECCA KAUFFMAN

COUNTERPOINT · CALIFORNIA

THE RESERVATION

This is a work of fiction. All of the characters, organizations, and events portrayed in this novel are either products of the author's imagination or are used fictitiously.

First Counterpoint edition: 2026

ISBN: 978-1-64009-748-3

The Library of Congress Cataloging-in-Publication data is available.

Jacket design by Nicole Caputo
Jacket photograph © iStock / heinstirred
Book design by Laura Berry
Wine stain © Adobe Stock / Aleksey

COUNTERPOINT
Los Angeles and San Francisco, CA
www.counterpointpress.com

Printed in the United States of America

3 5 7 9 10 8 6 4

for Jack Shoemaker

MENU

THE RESERVATION

THE OPERATIONS ASSISTANT

THE LATE OCTOBER AIR WAS BLUE AND COLD. Frost glittered on the paved lot of the apartment complex. Danny deadbolted the door behind him, crossed the lot, made a left, and walked along the shoulder of the quiet street until he reached the Dollar General, where the sidewalk began. He breathed into his cold fists then stuffed them into the pockets of his fleece. His knuckles met crumbs. He passed the poultry plant. It was already spewing smoke and filling the air with a strong meaty smell. He approached the railroad tracks, where a grimy pink Popples toy lay face down directly on the rail. He toed it out of harm's way. The sky was still starry overhead but pale to the east.

Danny's key worked only on the basement door, not the front entrance of the restaurant that faced the street and displayed the name—*Aunt Orsa's*—in fat, looping cursive.

That main door would remain locked until either Chef Oz or Rhea, the manager, arrived. Danny entered, clocked in, and turned on the lights. The restaurant smell lived on his clothing but was still briefly overpowering upon each arrival. He dropped his fleece in his locker and retrieved his clipboard then went upstairs to the kitchen to start coffee.

There was a note from Orsa on the dry-erase board next to the schedule relating to tonight's service: *IT'S GRISHAM DAY, PEOPLE. No staring, no small talk. Carpe diem. —AO*

Orsa wanted the staff to address her as "Aunt O"—*I'm everyone's favorite crazy aunt,* she insisted—even though Danny was her only actual blood relation at the restaurant, and of his two aunts she was not his favorite. She was crazy, though.

Danny had come here to work for her six months before. Orsa had created the role of operations assistant specifically for him—there was never consideration toward putting him on the line or behind the bar. Instead, Danny's job was essentially to look over shoulders. Double-check that closing duties had not been fudged. Cross-reference sales reports with inventory. General housekeeping oversight in common areas such as staff restroom and lockers. Danny reported infractions and Orsa addressed them. Danny liked the nature of the work, which made use of his eye for detail, and allowed him to move at his own pace. He liked arriving early and rarely overlapping with more than the same few people unless he really milked the clock into the afternoon. He did not like being a tattletale, but figured coming on as the owner's nephew with no prior restaurant experience, he never really stood a chance at making friends anyway.

Tuesdays were Danny's busiest shift of the week since the restaurant was closed on Sundays and Mondays, and Saturday nights were always slammed. It was the only fine dining establishment in their small town, which was home to a large university. Fall was the most hectic season between move-in weekend, Parents' Weekend, Homecoming Weekend, and football. Tuesday dinner service was usually relaxed compared to the weekend, but there was pressure today to have things primed for perfection because it was Grisham Day. It was only a ten-top, but Orsa would go berserk if anything went wrong at the famous author's table.

Danny waited for the coffee machine to sputter to completion then poured himself a cup.

He started his rounds. First, he checked that all of the essential machinery was functioning: ice machine, range, coolers and freezers at the proper temps. He slipped on a smear of oil next to the walk-in and wiped it up. Then he made his way through the restaurant, inspecting Saturday's closing side work. He wrote up that oil spill and a rack of unpolished wineglasses. He wrote up a toilet that was uncleaned and unflushed, and propped the restroom door open with the rubber stopper to dispel the stink. Near the staff lockers in the basement he discovered an unwrapped Twix bar on the ground. Food left out in the open like this over the weekend was among the worst infractions—Orsa had lamented to Danny on his first day about past rodent infestations. "Somehow we've still never gotten caught," she added.

"By a health inspector?"

"Or a guest. We've been close. A lady pointed across

the dining room one night, told Rhea it looked like a dead mouse. Rhea had the presence of mind to walk right over, pick up the thing with her bare hand, and carry it off without batting an eye. She reported back to the lady that it was just a mitten."

Danny tossed the Twix bar into the trash, added it to his report, and started inventory next. He worked his way through the bar and the kitchen and ended with the walk-in cooler. He checked the dates on the cartons of cream. He checked for mold on the wheels of cheese and bunches of beets with veiny, wilted greens. He checked for torn cellophane or discolored spots on the pork chops.

Because Chef Oz made orders and accepted deliveries throughout the week it was rare that any product was completely gone, so Danny was surprised to see that the shelf space designated for rib eyes was nearly empty—there were only two remaining, red and gleaming in their vacuum-sealed individual packs.

Served with spinach and polenta, the sixteen-ounce rib eye was the most expensive item on the menu. Danny had never seen fewer than a dozen of them in the walk-in cooler at any given time and usually it was many more. He wondered if Saturday night could have possibly been busy enough to clean them out.

He stepped out of the cooler to warm up while he looked back and forth between sales reports and the inventory he'd taken earlier in the week.

He did math in his head then with a calculator just to make sure and got the same result: Where there should have been twenty-four rib eyes, there were instead two.

He looked around for a note of explanation.

He poured himself another coffee.

In Danny's time as operations assistant there had been only one incident of potential theft, a huge box of toilet paper gone missing from the closet that housed paper products. Orsa wanted Danny to call her immediately in the event of inventory discrepancy, so he had that day, to report the missing toilet paper. Five minutes after he'd made the call, though, he found the box in the pantry, where someone had used it as a step stool. To avoid another false alarm like that one, Danny decided to do one more round through the entire place before calling.

When this search turned up no additional rib eyes, Danny went to the host stand and dialed his aunt from the restaurant phone, where he could also access the floor plan.

She picked up after a few rings. "What's up, kid?"

"We're missing rib eyes."

"What?!"

"Almost all of them; only two left. We're missing twenty-two."

"You checked everywhere?"

"Yes."

"On Grisham Day! What do we make of that?" Orsa puffed air loudly and it crackled into the earpiece. Danny could picture the expression on her face. Orsa resembled Danny's mother—petite, olive-toned, large eyes—but everything about Orsa was sharper, from the shape of the nose to the manicured nails. "Well," she said, "we'll pick some up at Giant before service, hopefully they've got plenty. How many are on the books total?"

"Forty-two," Danny reported. "Grisham ten-top, a pharma dinner twenty-top, and some deuces."

"We might need to hit Walmart too; you know those doctors and their red meat. Any theories about the theft? Leaving two almost seems like more of a statement than just taking them all, doesn't it? What about the busboy who always looks at me like he's holding in spit-up? Goes by some nickname. What do you know about him?"

"Ant? I hardly ever cross paths with him. From what I hear, servers love him, say he's a hustler."

"What about the Amish girl? She's the newest hire, right? I hate having new people around. Do you get the feeling she resents me?"

Jane was Mennonite, not Amish. She'd been hired several months ago, after the last pastry chef walked out with no notice. Orsa was on vacation at the time and left the rehire in the hands of Chef Oz, who reached out to Jane based on the recommendation of a friend, a wedding planner who spoke highly of Jane's cakes. Staffers had been taken aback to find the tattooed pansexual replaced by a girl in a bonnet—or a covering, as it was apparently called—but by all accounts Jane was doing a fine job.

Orsa repeated, "You think she'd do it? The Amish? You never know about those people. My friend's kid got involved with one of them and come to find out after a few dates, the girl had dentures. Horse kicked all her teeth in when she was ten. They've got their secrets, is what I'm saying."

"Not her," Danny said. Jane's round face flushed from the slightest bit of heat or effort or embarrassment. When things went wrong she said things like, *Land's sakes*. "Anyway," he continued, "the steaks must have been there for dinner service or you'd have heard before now. And Jane's usually long gone by then."

"Nobody would've noticed if she popped in later during dinner service for some reason, with the right excuse. You can't just start making assumptions about a person's character, Danny."

Danny fiddled with the cord of the phone and gazed to his left, into the dining room, where the morning sun cast sheets of ashy white through the narrow windows.

"Well," Orsa said, "I'm gonna get myself together and come in there to talk to everybody as they arrive. Rattle some cages. Do me a favor, give the restaurant one more good top to bottom, would you?"

Danny hung up then peered through the swinging door of the kitchen before entering, surprised to see that Jane had already arrived and was getting settled at her station, the brushed-steel counter gleaming before her. She tied her apron. The cinch of the strap around her waist was one of very few suggestions of an actual body attached to her head. Nearly everything else was covered or obscured except for the few inches of bare calf that were sometimes visible between the hem of her long, flowered dresses and the tops of her white ankle socks. Jane was pale and plump and unbearably beautiful.

She startled at Danny's entry. "I'm early because my driver's on a different schedule today," she explained. "One of the other girls had to be somewhere by ten."

A man in a tan Oldsmobile Cutlass dropped Jane off and picked her up every day. Danny had never gotten a good look but wavered between vague and acute jealousy.

"So he drives other people around, not just you?"

Jane nodded.

"How's a person land that gig?"

Jane went to the sink to wash her hands. Over her shoulder, she said, "He used to be part of the church. Left on good terms. Just wanted a different kind of life. He still works some hours at a dairy farm with his brothers and makes extra money chauffeuring people in the community."

"You can leave your church on good terms?"

"We don't shun, if that's what you're referring to. That's an Old Order thing. And even with them it's not as strict as it once was."

She poured herself a coffee, looked at Orsa's note, and stared into her PAR sheet and recipes. "What's on the books, other than Grisham?"

"Pharmaceutical twenty-top," Danny said. "A new rep. They'll all get dessert even if they barely touch it. They spend like you wouldn't believe."

"Seated on the patio, I imagine? So nobody's gonna want ice cream." Jane made a note and sucked on her teeth which were too flawed to be dentures, small teeth with spaces between them like a toddler's.

Pharma reservations always took place on the covered patio (which was heated, but still chillier than indoors once the sun was down), since privacy was a stipulation. The servers had stories about these events, which might involve large-scale anatomical models of a knee or a testicle. The drug rep would bring her own AV setup, wear stilettos, and drink Diet Cokes all night. The doctors would eat steaks and drink scotch or Cabernet.

Jane said, "And the Grisham ten-top of course."

"Are you a fan of his books?" Danny asked.

"Haven't read a single one. Don't usually care for mysteries."

"Why?"

"They're unpredictable," Jane said. "Or predictable."

Danny laughed.

He always tried to time his duties so that he would be in the kitchen for the duration of the time he overlapped with Jane. He especially savored the few minutes they had to themselves before Edgar the prep cook arrived. Once Edgar was there, the pleasant chitchat would be replaced by a barrage of self-aggrandizing tales and raunchy jokes. It was clear Edgar went out of his way to scandalize Jane with talk of late nights and heavy drinking, and sordid tales of dinner service relayed by front of house staff: the young mom who ordered a bowl of Caesar dressing for her son's dinner—*"Just charge me like it's soup"*—and the bar regular, an elderly woman, who always offered Darius the bartender a twenty-dollar bill to stir her cocktails with his bare finger.

Edgar wore a gold necklace and lots of product in his black hair. His physique was enviable despite his claim that he ate fast food exclusively. It occurred to Danny that he would not be unhappy at all if Edgar was revealed to be the thief of the steaks and took his leave, although that was highly improbable because, like Jane, Edgar's shift ended long before dinner service.

Jane said, "What's Grisham doing in town anyway?"

"Something with the university. Apparently he's doing speaking events on campus, then they'll end the day here."

"I imagine they'll all order dessert if it's on the school's tab. I'd better double brûlées." Jane peered into her refrigerator.

"Probably so," Danny agreed.

Jane headed toward the stairs leading to the basement and Danny followed her. He knew she was going for a forty-pound bag of flour, which was too much to carry on her own. She always protested when he offered help, insisting, "Not heavy, just awkward."

They hoisted it back up the stairs and to her station together. She sliced into it with a paring knife, creating a cloud, and transferred it to several large canisters.

Danny pretended to examine the range. He flipped a few switches, took some notes.

He contemplated telling Jane about the missing steaks but recognized it could be sabotage if she didn't react with genuine surprise when questioned later.

On her first day at the restaurant, while familiarizing herself with the menu, Jane's eyes grew wide at the price of entrees. She asked Danny if he'd ever had the rib eye and if it was worth the price tag, and Danny replied that he didn't care much for red meat, which was both true and only a fraction of the truth.

Several years before, Danny's mother had visited an urgent care center for dizziness and was told she was anemic. The nurse offered recommendations and advised a follow-up. They loaded up on red meat at Smart Shopper. Several weeks passed, and his mother weakened. She was a house cleaner, reluctant to cancel her appointments because she was afraid she might lose her clients, so she pulled

Danny out of high school (where he was a junior) and sent him in her place. His biggest surprise was not how wealthy his mother's clients were—although that was a surprise—but how hard she must have been working to complete everything on her list in the time she allotted.

When her strength did not return, Danny begged her to pursue that follow-up appointment, but she insisted they try harder with the meat first. She said they ought to exhaust all their options before scheduling another appointment; the first had cost more money than she made in a week. She made just enough money cleaning houses to edge herself out of Medicaid eligibility, but not enough to afford decent insurance. She reminded Danny that the nurse had said it could take weeks or even months to consume enough iron to make a discernible difference.

Danny could still remember the appearance of their refrigerator for the months that followed. Stacks upon stacks of ground beef and chuck cuts arranged by sell-by dates, some still in its packaging, some cooked and in Tupperware. Danny worked hard to make the beef appealing, seasoning and preparing it every possible way he could think to. He got creative with scrambles, stews, and stir-fries.

After these efforts and with no improvement to her health, his mother finally agreed to return to the urgent care center. There were tests and referrals and finally, a diagnosis of leukemia. The medical debt for treatment would of course bankrupt them, and they were told this was actually a lot more common than you'd think.

Because Danny's father was no longer in the picture and Danny had no siblings, he became his mother's full-time carer, driving her to and from appointments and the pharmacy and support groups, taking notes at each scan and update, administering medication, doing what he could to help her manage side effects, keeping the house up.

She lived for longer than they thought she would at the time of the diagnosis.

But in the end, she did die.

At her service, Danny overheard one of her hospice volunteers comment to another: "Must be a relief, in a way. Poor kid can get on with his own life now."

Danny was not so much insulted by this suggestion as he was genuinely bewildered by the phrase and concept of "his own" life.

Back in the kitchen, Danny straightened the spice shelf. He said to Jane, "Do you ever think about leaving?"

"No, do I seem unhappy? I try not to complain. I'm lucky to have the work, with the recession."

It was 2013—years past the onset of the housing crisis, but the job market had yet to recover.

"Not this job; your church. Because I'm just thinking about your driver," Danny said. "How you said he left the church but still works with his brothers and gets to hang out with you and your friends, still gets to be part of things as much as he wants. Right? But I imagine he doesn't have to follow the rules anymore. He's allowed to drive obviously. And have a drink, I imagine. Date whoever he wants. Dress however he wants."

What Danny meant to say was, *I'd be willing to join your*

church in order to marry you, but it might be easier if you were willing to leave your church in order to marry me.

Jane didn't really seem to be listening to the things he was saying or not saying.

Danny was so madly in love with Jane it was like a cramp in his brain. Before Jane arrived at the restaurant, he was in love with Kenzie the server until he overheard her making fun of the way his pants fit to another server. Danny was mortified. He didn't have a clue how pants were supposed to fit, if not the way his pants fit. Before Kenzie, it was the girl who worked at the 7-Eleven where Danny routinely bought Gatorade and taquitos; before that it was the sad-looking mom who often passed his home jogging behind her stroller; and before that, the woman who gave the local weather forecast on the radio, whose face he'd never seen.

DANNY WATCHED AS Jane measured olive oil by the cupful and tossed it into the mixer for focaccia. Ordinarily Danny would stick around a while longer, but he decided to hit the road early today—he didn't want to be here for Orsa's arrival and the line of questioning about the steaks that would follow.

He went down to the basement to retrieve his fleece and keys.

Before he opened his own locker, Danny's eyes fell on Jane's locker, which was slightly ajar. He peered in through the open inch, enough to notice that it contained more than she typically carried. He eased it open a little farther to get a better look. The small pink and green purse that always traveled with her hung from a hook, and beneath that rested a large, zippered canvas bag. The zipper was only partially shut, and Danny could see through the sliver that there was denim inside. At first glance, this struck him as totally normal—various staff members wore street clothing and changed into uniforms or kitchen scrubs upon arrival—but then it occurred to Danny that Jane didn't have a uniform; she simply arrived, worked, and left, in her flowered Mennonite dresses. Furthermore, he'd been under the impression that she was not allowed to wear jeans, ever.

Danny walked to the stairway and peered up it to make sure he had closed the door at the top behind him and would have ample warning if she happened to come down. Then, he returned to her locker, opened it farther and unzipped the canvas bag nearly the whole way. He sifted his hands through to view the contents: a pair of women's jeans, a cardigan, and a ratty baseball cap that read *Tampa Bay*. Articles of clothing that Jane would not, could not, wear. Danny's thoughts were suddenly slapping about, to process this puzzling reality. There might have been more in the bag, but he was too spooked to explore.

He zipped the bag back up and closed the locker door most of the way like it had been before.

He considered. Wouldn't it make more sense if it was the opposite way around—that Jane assumed a "normal" identity in the workplace to blend in for the duration of her shift, only arriving in the Mennonite garb and donning it just before pickup? This other version made no sense at all.

Which of the outfits was the disguise and why was it necessary?

Danny took a moment to compose himself before putting on his fleece and returning to the kitchen for one more slug of coffee and to bid Jane farewell, as he always did before clocking out.

He went up the stairs, rounded the corner, and observed her, his mind flitting down several alien paths.

When she registered his presence she looked up from the mixing bowl on the counter before her. "Have you heard anything about my cannolis? I'm worried my cream is too dense. Nobody ever tells me anything." She tapped a whisk against the side of the bowl.

Danny said, "Nobody ever tells me anything either."

He tried to picture her wearing the clothing that was in her locker. If he had dug deeper through that bag, he thought, alternating between despair and delirium at the possibilities, what would he have found?

As Danny contemplated the absurd notion that Jane was operating under a false identity and using it to enact mischief such as the stealing of the steaks, he realized he was so in love with her that even if that were verifiably the case, he'd never tell. He'd cover for her. He'd take the fall.

The more he thought about it, the more he realized how badly he wanted Jane to disappear into the basement right now, returning to the kitchen wearing jeans and a backward ball cap over long, loose hair, and carrying a zippered canvas bag heavy with twenty-two steaks.

She would beg him, "Run away with me, Danny, join me in my different life."

"I will follow you anywhere," Danny would say. "But you'll need your strength."

He'd insist she take a seat there on the counter, legs

dangling. He'd start up the grill. He'd offer her a glass of wine then toss the steaks onto the grill one by one. The meat would sizzle and spit. He'd watch for a good sear, flip them with tongs, and remove them from the heat as they came to temperature. He'd let them rest to hold their juices then stack them all onto a single heaping platter. Jane would follow him into the dining room and together they would sit at table number eight, the most requested two-top in the place, located in a corner and next to a window that offered both the feeling of privacy and a view. He'd sit across from Jane in her jeans and watch her devour three hundred and fifty-two ounces of steak; he'd leave the table only to bring her fresh napkins and to refill her water glass.

THE OWNER

ORSA WAS ON THE RECUMBENT BIKE WHEN Danny called about the steaks. After hanging up, she mulled over whether to shower and rush in there or finish the workout first. A quick response and presence in the restaurant following this sort of thing was important for asserting authority. But she was enjoying herself. After a night of rain the sun was sublime, the sky cloudless with the intensity of blue that you never got on a warm day. The bike was located in the guest bedroom on the second floor of their house and she had it faced out the large cathedral window, toward the street, so she could watch the neighborhood goings-on while cycling furiously. She had always been an amazing biker, ever since training wheels. Occasionally when the light was right, like this morning, walkers would catch a glimpse of her up there through the window, but they usually didn't wave back.

She toweled off her face and hollered for Larry in the direction of the staircase a few times until he appeared in the doorway of the room, damp and bent at the waist. The steps were hard but good for him. If it wasn't for Orsa he'd probably never leave the couch.

"Guess what," she said. "We've got a thief on our hands. On Grisham Day, of all the days."

Larry took a seat on the edge of the guest bed and pulled absently at a gold tassel on the bed runner. "Petty cash?" he said. "Booze?"

"Rib eyes. Twenty-two of them." She pointed at the tassel. "Leave that thing alone, you'll make it fray."

"What do you buy them at?"

"Little under ten apiece. So we're looking at a loss of two hundred, wholesale. Triple that if we're talking profit."

"What does a person do with twenty-two steaks? That's a hell of a feast."

"I can imagine a black market."

Larry screwed up his red face. "For meat? It couldn't possibly be worth the trouble for the hundred bucks you might make off-loading them. Although I guess a hundred bucks is a lot, depending on who you're dealing with. A car payment or a bunch of drugs. Dope. Smack."

Orsa cracked up at the way he said *smack*. Larry was retired now but had enjoyed an illustrious career as a personal injury lawyer—the only one in town—so he'd had some experience with the sort of people who worked for Orsa, though he'd never learned to talk about them in a way that wasn't categorically ridiculous.

Because of his work, Larry had been helpful when Orsa first opened the restaurant ten years ago, educating her on all the ways to safeguard against employee claims. He pointed out that as a female business owner, she was especially vulnerable to grifters looking for a quick buck. But aside from the occasional legal guidance, Larry was pretty hands-off with the restaurant, which Orsa appreciated. He had no input on menu or service or anything like that. He had the palate of a dog, she always said. Meats and treats.

"Is Danny the one who called?" Larry asked.

She nodded.

"What are the odds somebody misplaced them and he just hasn't looked hard enough? Or he bungled the numbers?"

"Wouldn't be like him," she said. "There are two left anyway, on the shelf where there should be twenty-four."

"Interesting. That seems more like it might be a statement then, leaving two. Any theories?"

"Haters, you mean? Half the people in there. The question is just which of them has the biggest balls and the thickest skull."

"With Grisham coming tonight, maybe you need me—"

"I told you, Lare, I don't want you around. No lurking, no autographs, don't even think about it. You can come for a quick glimpse at a safe distance, but that's all."

The most exciting people to set foot in the restaurant to date were a food blogger with six thousand Facebook followers, and a Nickelodeon child star (now in his twenties) who Orsa had never heard of. Oh, and the local weather man, who always asked for ice in his red wine. While it was exciting to see a TV personality in the flesh, he came so often that by now it ceased to cause a stir.

Larry scowled. "I was simply going to offer to do the

steak pickup so you can be a presence at the restaurant all day. With Grisham coming tonight and all."

"That would be great," Orsa said, wiping her face. "I'll call the supplier first, but I'm almost positive they won't be able to deliver on this short notice, so we'd better plan on you hitting the Giant. Pick up thirty-some, if they look decent. Don't lose the receipt. If they don't have enough, try Walmart. And plan on doing another once-over of the restaurant when you come for the drop-off. Sniff around all the corners."

Larry picked his nose. "Do you still just have the one surveillance camera?"

Orsa nodded. "In the bar. It captures the register but won't be any help on this."

"I keep telling you to install more," Larry pointed out.

"And I keep telling you I got in a fight with the guy who installed it, and I'll be damned if I give that company any more of my money."

Orsa eased herself off the bike and did a deep stretch. When she stood up, Larry was fiddling with the gold tassel again, so she swatted his hand like it was a bug.

ON THE DRIVE to the restaurant, Orsa went out of her way in order to pass Danny's apartment. He had no car, so there was no way to know where he was unless she passed him on his walk. She always offered rides, but he insisted he liked the fresh air.

He was nowhere in sight, therefore either already back at his apartment, or still at the restaurant. Orsa was hoping for the latter so that he could be part of the first few inquests, and perhaps she could even coax him into sticking around for all of them. She hadn't decided yet how she was going to conduct the questioning—if she would pull people into her office one by one or what. Either way, it would be nice if Danny was there, to sit on her side of the table.

Back when Orsa's sister Lorene called to inform her that it was a matter of weeks or days, not months, that she had left, Lorene begged Orsa to look after Danny, to help him clear their apartment, move him to Orsa's town, which was several hours away, get him a fresh start there, provide him with work and a place to stay if need be. *See, he hasn't even got his high school diploma*, Lorene reminded her sister, and it was no small task nowadays to break into the workforce. Orsa promised.

It was a heartbreaking ordeal, Lorene's illness. And Lorene had refused help, financial or otherwise, all along, right up until the end, this business with looking after Danny. Orsa would have helped with money if Lorene had asked. They never talked about money. It wasn't a sore subject. It wasn't Orsa's fault she'd married rich; it wasn't Lorene's fault she hadn't. There was another sister, the youngest, who was still free-spiriting out in California and was unlikely to marry at all.

In any case, after that phone call with her sister, Orsa developed this cushy job for Danny at the restaurant, a win-win deal. The work itself would be straightforward and easy enough for someone without a diploma, and the nature of the job provided justification for her to pay him well since it was management adjacent. It would benefit Orsa to have a family member—someone she could trust implicitly—in this sort of a role. And hopefully his presence would help keep people in line. They'd be less likely to loaf about if they knew the owner's nephew was around.

When she posed this plan to Larry, he said, "Everybody'll hate the kid, coming in as a glorified snitch. Sure you don't want to start him on dishes?"

Orsa said, "He's done enough dishes, Larry. And he doesn't need friends. He needs me."

"A paycheck?"

"A family."

ORSA ENTERED THE restaurant through the basement, came up the stairs, and approached the door to the kitchen as quietly as possible. She liked taking her employees by surprise.

She swung the door open to see Edgar and Jane standing together at the coffee machine with their backs to her.

She observed that there was a stockpot simmering and brûlée assembly taking place but still said, "Any work happening in here or are we just enjoying the free coffee?"

Jane spun to face Orsa right away, cheeks surging with pink.

Edgar was slower to acknowledge her. He sipped his coffee. "Just refueling. Is that alright, Big Enchilada?"

Orsa had no clue why Edgar called her that sometimes. Everybody was big next to Edgar, who was about five-two. But he had a muscular build and appealing swagger. And Chef Oz claimed Edgar was very efficient despite the chitchat and the hangovers, so there was plenty to appreciate about him.

Jane returned to her station and Edgar returned to the stove. He stirred his sauce then delivered Orsa a taste from the reddened tip of his wooden spoon.

"No thank you," she held up her hand. "I just brushed my teeth."

When Jane's eyes darted to the clock Orsa clarified, "I brush after every meal."

She gazed down at Jane's brûlées, which looked perfect. Her desserts were tidier and more consistent than the previous pastry chef's. But Orsa could not get past the Mennonite thing—the idea of a woman dressing that way, like there was no inherent power in being a female with a body—as if they were above all that.

Orsa for one didn't leave the house without lipstick and loud prints, cleavage on display. Naturally, she still caught guys half her age—like Edgar—checking her out. What a waste, she thought, to look like Jane and dress like a hobo from the 1920s.

Edgar said, "What brings *you* in this morning? Free coffee? Or just excited for Grisham Day?"

"Since we're talking freebies," Orsa replied, "I might as well get right into it. Danny called this morning."

Edgar and Jane both paused their work to focus on her. Danny's name carried weight around here. It usually meant someone was about to get a scolding.

Orsa grabbed the reading glasses that lived on a beaded chain around her neck to place them on her nose.

She said, "Is he here?"

"Danny?" Jane said. "He left maybe thirty minutes ago."

Orsa shoved off a pang of disappointment.

Edgar said, "What's going on? Something about Grisham?"

"Theft," Orsa announced, pausing to gauge their reactions.

Edgar whistled a slow arc. "Of what?"

"Rib eyes. Twenty-two of them."

Edgar laughed then stopped. "Really? That's weird, yo."

Orsa said, "Tell me about it, *yo*," exaggerating the lilt in Edgar's speech. "Even weirder is they left two behind."

Jane had stopped working. She wiped her sugary fingers on her apron and sipped from a glass of water. "You think it was a staff member?"

"There's no one else with access." Orsa looked back and forth between the two of them.

Edgar said, "The hell's somebody gonna do with all of that meat?" His marinara sauce bubbled, and he turned the heat down.

Orsa said, "How would I know? Throw a party? Larry and I discussed the possibility that someone stole them for money to off-load them way below cost. Made a hundred bucks or something. Seems like a risk and a rigmarole to me for a hundred bucks, but what do I know? Although I think I pay well enough that nobody's *that* hard up." She took her glasses off to give them a quick wipe on the hem of her shirt, then put them back on.

Edgar said, "Hundred bucks is a hundred bucks. Times are tough. But like you said, there'd be easier ways. Also, leaving a few behind makes it seem vindictive or something, no?"

Orsa nodded in agreement. "Especially it being Grisham Day and all. Now, I'm not a dummy, I know not everyone that works here is an angel. I actually pride myself on that, you know. Giving people second chances.

Did you guys know that Willis has a felony on his record? I still hired him." When neither of them responded she said, "Okay, how about a hunch? Anybody rubbing you the wrong way?"

"Nobody rubbing me any kind of way," Edgar said. "Unfortunately." He stuck his tongue out the side of his mouth and laughed. Jane laughed, too, turning her head to bury her red face in her shoulder.

Orsa said, "Be serious for a minute. Do you know of anyone in money trouble? Addicted to drugs? What do you think? Or is anybody mad at me about something? Come on, *think*."

Edgar reached for a cutting board. "Grisham's the mystery guy, ain't he? Why not put him on the case?"

"You think you're the first one to think of that joke?" Orsa said. She was starting to get bored, so she turned to Edgar and took several strides toward him, until she was close enough to reach out and finger the gold necklace around his neck. "This new?"

"Gift from my Granny. I've had this thing since I was a kid."

"You must be Granny's favorite."

"I am," he retorted.

"I'm just giving you a hard time," Orsa clucked. "I know it wasn't you. You love me."

She wondered if Edgar's grandmother gave all of her grandchildren gold jewelry and told all of them they were her favorite. That was the kind of grandmother Orsa thought she would be, back when she thought she would be a grandmother, or a mother.

Orsa was in her mid-twenties when she and Larry married, and they didn't stop trying to have a baby until she was in her mid-forties. It made her head spin to think back on those years now, because to her memory, for that time spent trying, she did not have one single thought about one single thing other than the trying. Decades of life devoted to the one thing and ultimately it was a net zero.

Initially when it didn't happen Orsa assumed it was Larry with the bad sperm—he was a good deal older than her and didn't take care of himself. But the doctor said Larry's sperm was actually just fine and so were Orsa's eggs and other features as far as they could tell. It just didn't happen, and didn't happen, and didn't happen. Doctors insisted sometimes there was no medical explanation—it just didn't happen. Orsa thought, *Okay, but it will happen.*

When Orsa turned forty-four, the night sweats started and she knew it was over.

She lay in bed for a week feeling such immense grief and relief simultaneously it was like she was swallowing one entire life and being swallowed by another one.

When she finally got out of bed, she told Larry she wanted to open a restaurant and he said, "How much do you need?"

Orsa's mother hailed from Long Island, the oldest of eight, and at a young age she had been put on kitchen duty, often preparing meals for the whole family so her mother could tend to other tasks. They ate simple, sturdy, starchy Italian fare. Pasta with red sauce, polenta with cheese, oily potatoes, lentils with sugar and celery. Leftovers got tossed together into new bakes or stews. Cheap cuts of meat were incorporated when available. Orsa's mother passed this style of cooking on to her own daughters, so Orsa was exposed to these flavors and techniques early, and of her sisters she was the one most keen to spend time in the kitchen.

When Orsa's mother eventually became ill, Orsa got her mother's input in recording all of the family recipes in writing, and after her mother died, Orsa spent countless hours mastering them.

Larry's uninspired palate disappointed Orsa. He wasn't exactly unappreciative. But he didn't have a clue. Orsa consoled herself with the idea that their future children would appreciate her cooking even if their father didn't; that their children's friends would beg for dinner invites.

Orsa's culinary sensibilities expanded with travel in the early years of marriage. She pushed for New York City, New Orleans, Europe. Larry had already done plenty of travel by the time they met and would have probably preferred to just swan around the deck of a Carnival Cruise ship with his belly out, eating Froot Loops, but Orsa had a thirst for culture. She was enchanted by paella, falafel, crepes and quiches, beignets, jerk chicken, black pudding, bread pudding, chowders, dumplings, currywurst.

When the time came to devise her menu for Aunt Orsa's, she drew inspiration from all over the world while highlighting her mother's recipes. This meant that the restaurant did not fall easily into any one type of cuisine. In its first review, the local newspaper described it as "offbeat, eccentric Italian-ish." Because they had positive things to say about every dish they tried, that description suited Orsa just fine.

EDGAR HAD GOTTEN out a cleaver and was processing purple cabbage for the slaw they served with the bacon appetizer. It was mesmerizing to watch him chop, the delicate flakes of purple and white stacking in neat mounds next to the shining blade.

When he went to the basement to retrieve some fennel, Orsa left the kitchen, not wanting to be alone with Jane.

She went to her office, opened her computer to look over sales reports, and stared at the blue screen while Microsoft slowly performed updates. She didn't need the updates; didn't want them. Apparently, she didn't have a choice.

She gazed at the fake orchid that lived on top of her filing cabinet. It looked great in the afternoon when she typically arrived, but fuzzy and stupid now in the direct morning sunlight. She wondered if people made fun of it.

She knew she should be grateful to Danny for being so efficient that he clocked out before eleven, even on a Tuesday—she didn't get the feeling he ever milked the clock. He was a good worker. A good kid. At the same time, she was so hoping he'd still be here so that they could confer about the theft and come up with a game plan together. She had even thought she might let him be the one to confront the thief if he wanted to.

Was it worth giving him a call to see if he'd come

back in? She could offer to pick him up at his place so he wouldn't have to do that long walk twice in one day.

AFTER LORENE HAD called requesting Orsa's help looking after Danny once she was gone, Orsa had gotten to work on the basement of her and Larry's home. It was suitable for a guest and had its own private entry but was not particularly inviting, and definitely not decorated right for a guy his age. Orsa had updated the bedroom décor and fashioned the rest of the space into a rec center, purchasing a Ping-Pong table and some framed sports memorabilia. It had a kitchenette, and Danny would of course be welcome to come upstairs to use her and Larry's full kitchen any time. Perhaps they would make some traditions, she thought, like pancakes on Sunday mornings.

But after Lorene's service, when the time came to actually get Danny back on his feet and moved, while he happily accepted Orsa's job offer, he declined her invite to stay in their basement free of charge. She'd said, *But it has its own entrance.* She did not mention the pancakes. Danny thanked her but said he'd prefer to look for an apartment with roommates his own age, try to make some friends that way since he was new in town.

The rejection was staggering to Orsa. She didn't let Danny see it, but Larry saw it. He said, "He's just proud, like his mom. Stubborn. Not going to accept any more help than what he absolutely needs." Larry tried to convince her that, bigger picture, it was much better to have a nephew like this than some wastrel. Larry said, "Besides, the basement renovation won't go to waste. My brother's kids will love it down there if they come for Christmas."

ORSA PICKED UP an old *Bon Appétit* magazine. Most of the recipes used by the restaurant were set in stone, but sometimes she paged through food magazines for ideas on a modified presentation, or a weekend special she could suggest to Chef Oz.

When the magazine failed to interest her, she did the thing where she shimmied her glasses the whole way down then back up the bridge of her nose without using her hands. The Microsoft updates were complete by the time she had finished.

Before opening sales reports she clicked her long fingernails on the desk and stared at the framed photo that lived next to the pen cup. It was a black-and-white shot of her and Lorene and their younger sister when they were all teenagers, looking breezy and gorgeous. The first time Danny saw the photo in here, he said, pointing, "Is that my mom?"

Orsa stared at him, thinking at first he must be joking, then she realized he was not.

"No," Orsa said. "That's *me*." She pointed back to the photo. "And *that's* your mom."

DANNY HAD ENDED up in a shitty Craigslist apartment with three roommates. It was located past the Dollar General on the wrong side of the tracks. The day Danny got his keys and Orsa accompanied him in the U-Haul, she poked her head in. It smelled so strongly of piss and patchouli she actually gagged. Danny said, "You said you needed to use the restroom?"

Orsa coughed and turned back to the U-Haul. "On second thought, I'll chance it."

Later that day, Orsa got cocktails with her friend Linda. She was going to tell Linda about that horrendous apartment but didn't get a chance, because Linda started right in, tearfully reporting that her step-granddaughter, a two-year-old, had just died of a hole in her heart.

Orsa said, "That's weird."

Linda stared at her. "*Weird?* Jesus Christ, Orsa. The baby died. I think you mean *sad*."

Of course it was sad. You didn't have to say so.

Life was so full of misunderstandings. See, it wasn't weird to Orsa that the baby had died. Everybody died. It was weird that a person could live even one day, even one minute, with a hole in their heart.

THE PASTRY CHEF

Jane startled when Orsa entered the kitchen, even though Orsa couldn't possibly have overheard what Jane and Edgar were talking about. Jane was relieved when moments later Orsa explained about the steaks.

Hopefully the ruckus surrounding the theft, on top of the excitement of Grisham Day, would distract everyone from the change of clothing and quick exit Jane planned to make at the end of her shift today. Still, it was annoying to have Orsa around. Somehow Jane had managed to avoid a reprimand thus far in her time at the restaurant, but she knew it was only a matter of time because if it wasn't Orsa it was her nephew, Danny, who was always looking, always lurking.

Once Orsa had left the kitchen, Edgar snickered. "Black market for rib eyes?"

Jane finished pouring warm brûlée custard—cream,

egg, sugar, the fine black innards of one vanilla bean—into ramekins before answering. "Makes as much sense as anything else, doesn't it? Can you really imagine someone stealing that many just to eat?"

"I imagine they freeze well. You a fan of steak?"

"Not particularly." Jane used a spatula to collect the glistening yellow remains of liquid custard from the lipped bowl into one neat scoop, which she smeared onto her tongue. Edgar used to scold her about the raw egg, but he'd quit.

"Thought you were a meat-and-potatoes kind of girl," Edgar said.

"Are you saying I'm fat?"

"I'm saying, your family farms."

"But soybeans, mostly," Jane said. "No cattle." She walked through his station and preheated the oven.

Edgar finished chopping celery and used his knife to empty the large cutting board into the stockpot on the stove. He disappeared into the basement and returned with a bucket of onions and the comically large safety goggles he wore while chopping them. He had told Jane during her first shift that keeping your lips closed in the presence of onion chopping helped, too. Onion chopping was the only ten minutes of silence Jane got once Edgar arrived for his shift. But she rarely minded his chatter—his stories entertained her. And later today he was going to do her a favor that she wouldn't have asked of anyone who she didn't consider a friend.

After Edgar had finished the onions he took off his safety glasses and lit the range. He dumped oil, glugging from its jug, into a sauté pan.

Over the sizzling, he said, "So, where we going this afternoon?"

Last week Jane had asked Edgar if he would be willing to give her a ride to and from an appointment on a future date—today—after they both finished their shifts. She said it would take a few hours. She offered to pay for gas and his time. Edgar said he'd be happy to and wouldn't accept a dime.

She answered blithely, "Just an appointment."

"Is your usual driver taking the afternoon off?"

"Not exactly," she said, then realized there wasn't much point in trying to keep their destination secret any longer, since he'd be driving her there in a few hours. So she explained, "It's an appointment I don't want my driver to know about. Or the other girls he drives."

Edgar tossed a few whole cloves of garlic into the oil. "Now you've got me a little excited."

"It's to a doctor's office."

Edgar's chin jerked to his neck. "You people aren't allowed to go to a doctor?"

"A women's doctor."

"Oh, shit." He turned to face her and lowered his voice. "Girl, are you pregnant?"

"What? No," Jane snorted. "It's just for my health." She carefully arranged her ramekins on a deep roasting pan.

"I thought I was your boyfriend. Are you cheating?"

Jane laughed. Edgar made references like this all the time even though he had a serious girlfriend.

She said, "It's just a routine health thing." The oven beeped, indicating that it had reached temp. Jane poured a kettle of hot water into the brûlée pan for a water bath before covering the pan with foil, inserting it into the oven, and setting her digital timer for an hour.

"Tell me if I'm being too nosy," Edgar said.

"You are."

It was quiet for a bit while Edgar added onions to the sizzling oil, then readied his station for potato peeling. Eventually he whined, "Okay, but you've gotta tell me this at least. Are you leaving the church? Are you gonna let your hair down? I wanna be the first to know and the first to see."

"Oh my word. Don't look at me like that! I'm not... And I'm not... I haven't *done* anything."

"Am I the only person who knows about the appointment?"

"One other friend."

Jane turned on the mixer to cream butter, because it was too loud to talk over.

The friend was not exactly a friend, but she was the person who had prompted today's appointment, and the one who was planning on driving Jane until she had been called out of town for a funeral, hence the need for Edgar to drive instead.

PRIOR TO STARTING at the restaurant, Jane had sold sweets out of the farmers market, where her booth was located next to a midwife who sold homemade soap. The midwife was chatty, and somehow in the course of conversation, she mentioned that she'd worked with enough Mennonites to know it was taboo to show up at an OB's office if you were unmarried. But, she offered, it was medically advisable to have routine exams at a certain age, no matter what. She said, "I know you don't get taught this stuff in school." She said that she knew of several offices that did a sliding scale if you were paying in cash. Even though Jane found the midwife pushy and resented the powerful and unappealing scent of the woman's soaps—lavender, hemp, sandalwood—right next to her sweets, she ended up deciding she would like to have one of these routine appointments. The midwife was the one to call to get Jane scheduled and she offered to drive. Of course Edgar didn't need to know any of this.

But apparently his curiosity was not satisfied because once the mixer was off, he said, "How'd you make the appointment anyway, with the phone thing? I thought your whole huge family shared a landline. Were you nervous somebody would overhear? Or the office would call back to confirm?"

"My friend called from her cell to make the appointment. So, if they call back to confirm, it wouldn't be to my house." Jane covered her brûlées with a single sheet of foil.

Edgar was shaking his head. "You people make everything so hard for yourselves."

They had this conversation all the time; why Jane was allowed to ride in cars but not drive them. Why she was allowed to go to the movies but there couldn't be a TV set in the home. The phone thing. Et cetera. She knew she didn't owe Edgar any explanations, but she didn't mind. She preferred a person who would come right out and say it, or ask it, to a person who either addressed her like a small child or just stared, like Orsa; like Danny; like Byron, the server who often wrapped silverware in the kitchen, near Jane's station, instead of out in the dining room like the others.

It was quiet for a while, then Edgar said, "Do you think she's going to get the cops involved?"

"Who now? My friend?" Jane's mind was still on her appointment.

"Orsa. About the steaks." Edgar had finished peeling potatoes and was cubing them. "Say she figures out who it actually is. Will she just fire them, you think? Or get the cops involved, file a report and everything? You know how she likes to make an example. Or, say, she doesn't figure out who it is but gets herself so worked up she thinks she needs to call in the big dogs to investigate."

"She does get herself worked up, doesn't she?" Jane said. The oven beeped to indicate that it had reached temperature, and she slid the brûlées in. "You know her much better than me. But I can't imagine she'd want a cop traipsing through here, especially on Grisham Day."

Edgar dropped his knife then couldn't seem to locate his recipe book.

Jane watched him curiously. He routinely showed up with red eyes and the hunched back of someone who was not yet recovered from the previous night's antics. He always found his rhythm quickly, but Jane wondered now for the first time if Edgar was drinking on the job or if he had drugs stashed in his locker, which would account for his sudden interest in the possibility of a cop in their midst.

Her thoughts turned to their car ride later. She had no idea about the legal ramifications of, for example, being a passenger in a car if the driver was drunk, or if drugs were found in that car, or contraband such as stolen steaks.

Would Jane's name and her picture be put in the paper? Would the article say where their car had been headed at the time of the incident?

Edgar said, "What're the odds it was Kenzie who stole the steaks? That'd make for the best story. Don't you think?"

Kenzie the server was in a sorority at the local university. Apparently she was loaded, but her parents made her get a job after she'd nearly flunked out of freshman year. The deal was they would keep financing her education and her sorority membership and her wardrobe only if she proved she was responsible by getting her grades up and holding down a job for the remainder of her time as a college student. Kenzie, now a junior, had publicized this deal widely among the restaurant staff so there was no confusion about her relationship to the job and to the rest of the staff.

Jane pointed out, "She's skinny as a rail. I can't picture her eating half a burger, much less chowing down on a sixteen-ounce steak."

"Mm," Edgar grinned suggestively. "I can."

Jane retrieved several cartons of strawberries from the refrigerator, washed and trimmed and set them aside at her station. At the stove, she emptied a bag of baking chocolate into a saucepan and turned the heat on low.

Orsa reappeared in the kitchen, flushed with excitement as she announced: "The bank security manager's going to give me their footage. The Wells Fargo." Orsa pointed with her thumb in the direction of the small branch located next to the restaurant—they shared a parking lot.

Edgar wiped his chin onto his shoulder. "How's that gonna help?"

"My only security camera here is over the register in the bar but the bank's got one that faces us and spans the whole parking lot, all the way to the employee entrance. I just got off the phone with the shift manager who's going to isolate footage from Saturday and send it to me to review." She bent to look at her reflection in the chrome espresso machine. "I don't know if it'll be definitive," she said, "but it'll probably rule out some people. You have to be carrying a bag of a certain size if there's twenty pounds of meat in there. The bank guy said it'll be a little grainy but might give us some good intel." Her cell rang in her pocket, and she stepped out of the kitchen to take the call.

Jane helped herself to another coffee.

Edgar said, "So, this doctor's appointment. What happens if you run into someone you know there?"

"I brought some regular clothing so I can be incognito, on the off chance. Someone would only recognize me if they were really close and really looking."

"You thought of everything, didn't you? If you're going to change clothes here at the restaurant before we head out, you might want to do it a little early and be waiting in my car by quarter after. So you don't overlap with servers when they start rolling in."

"I guess you're right," Jane said.

"Especially Byron. You don't want him seeing you in regular clothes. Get him all excited."

"Does he have a thing for me?" Jane said. She had the impression Byron might find her attractive, based on the staring, but he barely said boo to her, and there were rumors about him and the host, Julia.

She spooned some shortening into the melted chocolate to give it a gloss, stirred, then retrieved the colander with her strawberries.

"A crush on you? Probably," Edgar said. "But I meant, more so that you don't show up in his novel wearing normal clothing and on your way to see the ladies' doctor."

Jane picked up a berry, dipped it into the chocolate, set it on parchment. "What novel is that?"

"The one he's writing about you."

Jane laughed. "Yeah, sure."

"You don't know? He really is."

Jane turned to eye him. "Are you being serious?"

"I thought you knew. He's always got those little notebooks with him." Edgar took off his latex gloves with a flourish of powder and tossed them into the trash can. "Now that I'm thinking about it though, I guess he only talks about it after you're gone for the day."

"I still can't tell if you're being serious."

"Deadass," Edgar said. "I really thought you knew."

"I know he writes."

"It's why he often comes in early," Edgar explained, "to overlap with you. And why he wraps silver back here instead of in the dining room. Trying to get more material. And he's always asking me what you and me talk about, since we work together all morning. Usually I can't remember."

Jane stared at Edgar, a strawberry suspended and dripping melted chocolate back into the saucepan.

"Relax," Edgar said. "I won't say a word about the doctor's appointment."

"A *novel*? How could he possibly—"

"Relax," Edgar said again. "It's not *all* about you. Plenty of the things he talks about have nothing to do with you. Stuff he came up with on his own or heard somewhere else. For instance, like the dog thing he was talking about a while ago. I'm assuming that didn't come from you."

"What dog thing?"

"Apparently he's working on a scene of a little Mennonite girl walking in on her father and older brother in the middle of something in the barn. The brother holding the dog still while the father shoves a pipe down the dog's throat. To stop it from barking." Edgar had moved to the sink and was talking to her over his back while washing his hands.

Jane's jaw fell open. "But that's not me. My father would *never*, and I don't even have an older brother! Byron doesn't know the first thing—"

"See?" Edgar interrupted her. He made his way to the dish pit for a clean cutting board. "That's what I'm saying—don't worry about it. Seems like he's just taking little bits of what he sees and hears in here, but mostly his own imagination or whatever. That dog thing sounds like some urban legend he ripped off the internet, right? Clearly just going for shock value. Don't be mad. I shouldn't have referred to it as the novel he's writing *about you*. I was mostly joking. Who knows. I really thought you knew about all of this, though."

Edgar took off his apron, which meant he was going to use the restroom.

Jane stood in silence over the melted chocolate.

She tried to force her mind away from what she had just learned, willing her thoughts instead to the missing steaks.

Twenty-two of them, was it? Jane considered how much it would please her, knowing what she now did, if Byron were found out to be the thief. On top of getting fired, she thought, perhaps his computer and his little notebooks would be confiscated, and he would get tossed in jail. Then, she imagined, the novel about the Jane he thought he knew would languish in his mind and be replaced by a new story about, say, a cellmate whose life was defined by something violent and unspeakable.

Jane heard footsteps and muffled conversation in the dining room—Orsa, she assumed, and the bank manager with the precious footage.

Jane thought how nice it would be if you could access a recording of your own life if necessary—not for entertainment or pleasure or anything like that, but simply to fact-check, like Orsa was doing.

How nice it would be, Jane thought, to have an account available in black and white, to tell you exactly what had been taken from you, and by whom.

BACK WHEN JANE had first met the soap-selling midwife at the farmers market, in what was probably an attempt to make Jane feel comfortable about being the only conservatively dressed woman there, the midwife immediately told Jane that she had plenty of experience with Mennonite women.

Jane said, "You mean with your work? Delivering their babies?"

The midwife nodded. "And I'll tell you something. They're not hard to pick out. Five minutes of laboring, and

I'd know if I was dealing with a Mennonite, with or without the head covering."

"Really?" Jane said. "How?"

"They never scream," the midwife said. "It's like they're incapable."

SOMETHING HAD BOTHERED Jane about that, even though she supposed the midwife meant it as some sort of compliment—or at the very least, an effort to convey that she understood, if not *who* Jane was, *how* she was.

Jane realized now that she was irritated by that statement because it was exactly the sort of thing a writer would say. A writer or some other type of fraud; someone who was comfortable putting forth an absolutely preposterous lie if it had a certain greasy sheen of truth to it.

Of course Mennonite women screamed! What an idiotic thing to say.

With or without the head coverings, they were women with voices—they just weren't necessarily using them the way you expected them to.

THE PREP COOK

EDGAR THOUGHT JANE MUST HAVE DECIDED THE idea of Byron seeing her in regular garb was scarier than the slim possibility of encountering someone from her community at the office, because she was still wearing her dress when he found her waiting in his car. She was, however, nervously clutching the baseball cap in her lap.

Edgar had done his best to clean things up earlier this morning, but the smell inside his '96 Honda Civic still appalled him. "Sorry about the stink," he said, climbing in. "Dead mouse or something."

"It just smells like you in here," Jane said.

"Ouch." Edgar dropped his apron into the back seat, crawled into the front, and handed her a small paper bag.

"What's this?" she said.

He glanced into the rearview mirror. "It's your lunchtime, ain't it?"

"My word, that's thoughtful," Jane marveled. "I didn't remember to pack myself anything. I would've perished."

"I thought you might forget."

Jane routinely complained of hunger throughout her shift. She often spoke of the afternoon meal she would devour as soon as she was home, where she seemed to favor easy comfort food like Crock-Pot barbecued chicken or cheesy casseroles or cinnamon rolls. Now and then, she said that she and her driver and the other passengers would conspire for a fast-food run, which tempted Edgar now, but he figured it was more important to be punctual to her appointment.

She unrolled the top of the crinkled bag and peered in. "Not a steak, is it?"

Edgar laughed.

"You devil," she said, pulling out a glazed donut wrapped in wax paper and two Slim Jims.

"Not fresh," he said. "I got it on my way in this morning. But hopefully still good. I remember you said they're your favorites. One of those jerkies is for me, by the way."

"I'm shocked you remember the things I say." She passed over a Slim Jim.

"Got it all up here." He tapped his temple. "You better hope I draw your name for Secret Santa at the staff Christmas party."

"There's a staff Christmas party? With Secret Santa?"

Edgar nodded. "I'm surprised she hasn't announced the date yet."

"It's only October."

"She locks it in early."

"I guess. Sounds like fun." Jane bit into the donut.

"It's not."

"Why?" Jane asked, wiping her lips.

"It's held at Orsa's house. She tries too hard, makes it awkward. No one knows how to be. I didn't go last year, but Chef Oz told me it was a nightmare. Apparently she got so butt-hurt when people started to trickle out early she stood on her porch screaming, '*But the invite said eight to* eleven*!*' She accused people of having secret plans for an after-party somewhere else."

"Did they?"

"Probably. Where we headed, by the way?" Edgar asked.

Jane had a set of directions handwritten on a piece of paper, which she unfolded. "I'm sure you've got the thingy on your phone but I figured I'd have this along too just in case."

"I think I'll go with my thingy," Edgar said. He passed her his phone, directed her to the Maps app, and showed her where to type in the address for the doctor's office.

While waiting for the directions to load, Edgar admired the tree line on the far side of the lot, where the leaves were darkening and curling at their edges but still boasting rich burgundy and deep gold striations.

Jane said, "It's telling me eighteen minutes."

Edgar unwrapped his Slim Jim and bit into it. He followed Jane's instructions from the GPS onto Jericho Street, which passed near the university but would avoid all of the crosswalks.

Above the horizon of downtown brick retail shops and offices, the sky was a lustrous robin's-egg blue.

Edgar's phone rang a moment later, and when Jane turned it to face him, the caller was identified as: *Boss Lady.*

Jane said, "Your girlfriend?"

"Orsa. Please don't answer."

"Why's she calling you from her cell phone?"

"I ain't got a clue."

Jane said, "I wonder what she wants. Sure you don't want to take the call?"

"Yes." Edgar felt a squeeze in his throat as it occurred to him that it could be relating to the footage provided by the bank.

The call went to voicemail, and a *ding* moments later announced a text.

Jane was looking at the phone, trying to find her way back to the Maps app, and when she saw the text she read it aloud. "Boss Lady says, *Call asap*. Bunch of exclamation points. Are you gonna call back?"

"Eventually."

If Edgar's recorded actions from Saturday were coming into question, this was not a conversation he wanted to have with Jane in earshot. He would return the call when she was in with the doctor.

Jane finished her donut and crumpled up the wax paper, scattering white frosting crumbs. She peered into the paper bag, and when she didn't find what she was looking for she said, "You got napkins in here?" Before Edgar could stop her, she had opened the glove compartment.

She peered in at the contents: a toothbrush, toothpaste, razor and shaving cream, bar of soap and stick of deodorant.

She jerked her whole upper body so it faced Edgar. He pretended not to notice but simply stared straight ahead.

"What's all this?" she said.

"For when I stay at my girlfriend's."

"Why don't you just keep your stuff there?"

He hit a red light and drummed his fingers on the steering wheel. "Okay, you got me. She's married."

"Married!"

"So, I can't leave my stuff sitting around her place. Feel me?"

"Married?" Jane said again.

Edgar immediately regretted the stupidity of the lie. Of course Jane was onto him already. She said, "So you take your stuff and shave at her house when you're trying not to leave a trace? That doesn't make any sense." Jane regarded him. "I don't care one way or the other. I just want to know why you're lying."

Edgar's mind settled on a partial truth that might conceal the full truth. "Alright. Well, you might as well know, I don't want you thinking the stink in here is just *me* anyway."

"What is it?"

"I don't have a girlfriend; I have a second job. Sometimes I shower there if I'm coming straight to Aunt O's."

"Oh." Jane removed the wrapping from her Slim Jim and took a bite. Edgar hoped that would be the end of the inquisition, but as soon as Jane swallowed, she started right in again. "So, no girlfriend, just another job. You poor thing, that's why you're always so tired. Why lie?"

"Last thing I want is a pity party."

"You would rather people think you're unprofessional, showing up looking like you haven't slept in a week and whining about hangovers? What is it, by the way, the stink? What's your other job?"

"Poultry plant."

"What do you do there?"

"What does it matter?"

"I'm just making pleasant conversation now."

"I debone."

Jane glanced down at the GPS on his phone to confirm their next turn. "Here after the library," she said. The digital wraparound sign outside the library displayed the time—2:28—the temperature—fifty-one—and an animated red maple leaf that expanded like a firework before disappearing to a dot.

"Deboning," Jane said, "just like you did with your dad when you were a kid, right? Didn't you say you deboned the fish he caught?"

Edgar nodded.

"What's your schedule like at the poultry plant?"

"Night shift. Seven to seven."

"My word. And you shower at the plant to be at the restaurant by nine. When do you sleep?"

"Sometimes I grab a little in the car at the restaurant before clocking in." He nodded toward the digital clock in his car. "And, now."

"Well, I feel plain awful then," Jane said. "You're heading in to work a second shift—"

"What did I tell you about the pity party? Knock it off." Edgar glanced at her. "You've got crumbs on your chin."

She wiped them with the back of her wrist. "You must be putting a lot of money away with the two jobs. Good for you."

"Good for me," Edgar said. The reality was that he didn't even have a savings account. Twice a month, he sent almost his entire earnings to his family back in Guatemala via money order. His family consisted of his parents, two sisters, and two nephews. Edgar made enough to feed them all.

"So if you don't live with your girlfriend," Jane said, "do you live on your own?"

"Yep."

For a while, he had lived with other Guatemalan guys who worked at the poultry plant, about ten of them stuffed into an old frat house. The arrangement was convenient and dirt cheap. But the owner of the home had decided to sell, the new owner decided to renovate, and several of the guys living there were undocumented, so they all went their separate ways.

Edgar had slept in his car for a few weeks, planning to squirrel away extra money for a deposit at a new rental, but then he got used to sleeping in his car, and saving on rent was that much more money for him to send to his family rather than cough up to some landlord.

The shower room at the poultry plant was not nice but it was sufficient. The trunk of his car was big enough to hold his work uniforms, pillow, blanket, and window coverings for the car. A fast-food diet didn't require a kitchen. He had a PO box at the local post office to receive mail. The parking lot at Walmart was a good place for sleep following his restaurant shift, and the large parking lot that the restaurant shared with the bank worked well enough for a quick morning nap—that is unless someone had reason to review surveillance footage from the area.

He'd have an excuse at the ready if Orsa confronted him about his early arrival to the restaurant and time spent in the car prior to his shift, but there was no guarantee she would leave it at that.

THEY PASSED THE sprawling new student housing development and everything that had arrived to accompany it: Walgreens, Starbucks, 7-Eleven, Crunch Fitness, Sharp Cuts Salon, Subway.

"So how did you end up here?" Jane said. "Initially you told me you came to the states to follow your girlfriend, otherwise you would have stayed and taken over your dad's fishing business. So, if there was no girlfriend . . ."

"My dad got injured and couldn't fish anymore. We knew guys making five times more here in agriculture, construction, whatever, than I could ever make back there. A friend of a friend was already at the poultry plant and sent word they were hiring."

"I thought you said your dad was really successful leading tourist charters—that's why your English is so good. You grew up tagging along on excursions with tourists and your dad wanted you to be fluent. So, wasn't he preparing you to take over eventually?"

"The industry was changing. For a while, he was the only one in our area doing what he did. But he was operating out of his little boat, no liability insurance, no fancy equipment or anything like that. A big commercial chartering company moved in nearby. By the time he injured his shoulder, business was slowing down anyway."

"That's a shame," Jane said. "I can't imagine being so far away from my family. Especially because you've said you're really close to your mom, right?"

It did not escape Edgar's notice that Jane was now taking him through all the information he had ever offered, posing each old tidbit as a new question, fact-checking his life story. Annoying as it was, Edgar supposed he deserved it. "Always been a mama's boy," he confirmed.

The two of them had a scheduled call every Sunday. His mother always harangued him about his love life. She was desperate for more grandchildren even if an expensive flight would be required to meet them. She said, "With your looks you must have to fight them off."

"I'm too busy, Ma," he said. "No time for girls."

Sometimes she urged him to quit one of the two jobs, arguing that the family could get by on less than he sent—which was far more, she claimed, than any of her friends were receiving from their sons in the states. For Edgar, of course, it didn't matter how much he sent or how often he called; it would never be enough to dispel the memory that held him in its fist.

"You know," Jane said, "I've never been to the beach. I mean, my family's done weekends on the lake, but never the ocean. Is it magical and mysterious? That's how I imagine it. You ended up awfully landlocked here in the midwest," she pointed out. "Couldn't get much farther from the ocean if you tried."

It occurred to Edgar that when it came to oceans, the farther you ran from one, the closer you got to another.

He was eight years old when he had discovered just how magical and mysterious—or whatever—the ocean was.

Sweltering heat and the snoring of his sister wakened him and once he was alert he heard another sound, the creak of the screen door at the front entrance of their home. His bedroom window looked out onto the front lawn and he crawled out of his bed in order to see if it was somebody coming or going.

He watched as his father walked away from their home, wearing not the lightweight collared pajamas he slept in but cargo shorts, a T-shirt, and bare feet. His father's glossy ponytail gleamed in the moonlight and the muscles in his calves bulged with each step.

Edgar watched his father with awe as he reached the sidewalk and took a right toward the beach. Edgar was young enough that curiosity supplanted good sense. He crept out of the bedroom, through the house and out the front door to follow his father.

The hot air pressed on him, dense as a quilt.

Their home was located just a few blocks off the water and when the ocean breeze met his face, it was not cool but it had space in it.

Something told Edgar that he ought to stay out of his father's view even though he did not fear his father, who was always laughing. His mother was always singing; his father always laughing.

Edgar kept a distance from his father but could see when he headed toward the water, so he followed the sidewalk to its end where it met sand, which was loose and cool on his feet. The full moon lit his path and although his father had fallen out of his sight, it didn't take long before Edgar identified him out ahead, walking purposefully toward the wild night surf where whitecaps raged and silvery trails striated the dark sand.

Edgar crouched in a mess of beach grass. He watched

in a state of shock as his father walked into the water, fully clothed, until it met his waist.

Edgar brushed some beach grass from his cheek, where it stung. Facing toward the water, his father went still, posture rigid even as the surf pummeled him. His father's head turned left and right, searching.

Out of nowhere, fear overtook Edgar. He rose, hurtled over the sand and toward the water, desperate for the safety of his father, and he called to him, "Daddy, Daddy!"

At home they spoke only Spanish since his mother had not learned the language of the tourists. Elsewhere, Edgar's father encouraged English, and that was what made its way involuntarily up and out now.

"Daddy!" When Edgar neared the water's edge, his father heard him and looked Edgar's way.

His father smiled a sly smile then brought a finger to his lips and shushed. This motion coincided with the crashing of ocean surf, so that Edgar felt it vibrating all through his body: *Shhh, shhh.*

Edgar stayed where he was and watched, rapt, as his father stood perfectly still while a glittering fin suddenly appeared near him in the water, and when it drew closer his father pounced.

There was a great, wild wrestling, a flailing of limbs, his father's grunting voice.

His father gained control, and when Edgar squinted, even though his father was facing away from him, he could see that his father was clutching in both arms an enormous marlin that thrashed against him. Its head whipped back and forth, swordlike nose slicing the air, sparkling body strong.

Edgar choked on fear and wonder. He'd always known

his father was a hero—the way the women around town sang his praises and hung on his words. He'd just never quite imagined what that sort of heroism actually looked like, through his own eyes.

His father held the fish for a few seconds before releasing it, leaping back to give it room to flee, which it did right away. But before the fish was completely out of sight Edgar watched as its great caudal fin split into two bare legs, which kicked. And then it was gone.

Once the fish had fled the scene Edgar did, too, without a thought or consideration to the contrary. He ran back up the bank to the sandy path to the sidewalk to his house and back into his bed.

In the morning, the sand in his sheets was the only evidence that the whole thing had not been a dream. And even with the sand Edgar questioned the reality of the memory because his father made no mention of it at the breakfast table while he did his usual laughing and Edgar's mother circled the kitchen doing her usual singing, nor later in the day when he and his father were together at the beach, just the two of them, right at the site where it had occurred. But what was *it*? Something was terribly, terribly wrong about that fish.

Edgar desperately wanted to ask his father what he'd seen and what it meant, but he wasn't sure how to pose a question that wasn't childish.

He desperately wanted to talk to his mother but he didn't want her to stop singing.

The memory changed as time passed. Reality dissolved somewhat and entirely and oftentimes seemed to elude him to this day. Images morphed and replaced one another, moving in and out of view, and in and out of focus. That sparkling body, wrestled and released by his father, would not hold still in Edgar's mind. The feeling in Edgar's heart flipped and flopped. But the one detail that had never changed and in fact remained as clear to him now as the midday sun, was the image of his father's finger going to his smiling lips, and the shushing sound that accompanied the gesture. *Shhh, shhh.*

JANE INTERRUPTED EDGAR'S thoughts when the GPS directed them to turn into the parking lot of a large, nondescript brick office building with a list of doctors' names on a placard out front.

The lot was less than half full and Edgar picked a spot in the shade, hoping for a bit of sleep.

Edgar's phone dinged with the arrival of a new text and he glanced down to see Orsa had sent: *CALL ME! CALL ME. Don't make me beg.*

In the past, Edgar had always been able to come up with an excuse for not answering or returning an off-hours call, rare as they were. Would today be the day that Orsa made good on her threat to beg, or worse? In what capacity could she possibly need him so badly, right this instant? Presumably it had to do with the steaks; perhaps, specifically, the parking lot footage that showed Edgar sleeping in his car prior to his shift. Had Edgar's status relating to the theft already moved from confidant to potential witness to potential suspect? Sorely Edgar considered a defense: Living out of his car, he had no way to heat up a hot dog, much less twenty-two steaks.

Edgar turned the car off. When Jane didn't move to get out he looked her way and realized her cheeks were damp with tears.

"Uh-oh," he said. "Do you want to leave? I'll take you anywhere."

"No," Jane murmured, "I'm going to go in. I just feel . . . very far from my actual life." It was quiet for a bit. Eventually she said, "Will you walk me in?"

Edgar was so surprised and so moved by the request that for a moment he couldn't speak.

She added, "I know you need your sleep. You can come right back out." She pulled down the mirror flap and adjusted her covering. She turned to face him. "How do I look?"

Beautiful, he thought, and terrified; acutely, unmistakably real. This moment, he knew, would hold steady in his mind. He said, "Ready."

He looked back toward the building. A massively pregnant woman was exiting through double doors. She waddled with turned-out knees. Edgar could not tell from her face if she was in extreme pain or simply shielding her eyes from the sun.

Jane was watching her too. The woman hitched herself into the driver's seat of a tan minivan parked near them. Once she was in the vehicle, her entire posture changed, slumping with some emotion, and Edgar felt bad for bearing witness to this shift and the new emotion, whatever it was.

"Let's go." Jane's voice broke the silence as she pointed toward the entrance of the building with her chin. "From here to there. That's all it is."

Edgar thought it really didn't matter how much space

existed between *here* and *there*, or where your actual life existed on that spectrum, or who was at your side as you traversed it. See, the heart was a home with many rooms. And you would never stop relying on an impossibly complex network of truths, lies, and concessions to keep it all propped up and protected, like boards behind the walls, or bones within the body.

THE SERVERS

Rhea, Byron, and Kenzie were making their way through the dining room on opening side work. Kenzie was on silver and glassware, double-checking for dust and prints and tenacious lipstick stains. Byron was on napkins, folding them into clamshells and distributing on tables. Rhea was swapping old candles from the glass votives, using hot water. It was the least desirable task of the three because of the elbow grease required to wipe the smeary remnants. But Rhea was the lead server and floor manager, which meant an elevated hourly rate and her choice of sections. Since they didn't pool tips, this could mean the difference between a fifty-dollar shift and two-fifty. She always volunteered for the worst side work because she didn't need the other servers resenting her more than they already did.

Today was an exception to the normal course of things.

Orsa had approached Rhea back when the Grisham reservation was made, to make sure Rhea would be available to work that shift and serve that table. Rhea was not the prettiest or the most charming, but she was the most knowledgeable, the steadiest and most reliable. Rhea was not thrilled, exactly, to serve Grisham—whose books she'd never read—especially since it meant someone else would get the covered patio. Pharmaceutical dinners were a server's dream. The doctors ordered liberally, three courses were guaranteed because the rep would want all that time for her presentation, a 20 percent tip was added automatically, with several doctors likely to slip additional cash for no reason at all, and the rep would occupy the doctors' attention enough that they would be judicious with special requests. It was guaranteed two hundred at the low end and for minimal effort.

University parties on the other hand were a gamble, even with a bigwig at the table. The group might arrive with their budget in mind and be primed to limit the ordering, though that was less likely with a celebrity guest. They would definitely split off alcohol, tip 15 percent on food, and whether or not they would tip at all on alcohol depended on the person paying.

Rhea didn't know yet if Byron or Kenzie would be on the pharma dinner. If they both wanted it—which they almost certainly would—there would be a coin toss. The loser would handle normal reservations, mostly deuces tonight, which could always go either way, tip-wise.

They would make the final section determination after staff meeting, with Julia the hostess, since she'd be the one handling the flow, seating and assigning walk-ins.

Kenzie gingerly wiped a print from a glass and held it up to the light. "Did I tell you guys how my boyfriend wants me to try to buy Molly from Willis for Halloween weekend?"

"What is that?" Rhea said. "MDMA?"

Byron piped up from the table he had taken as his napkin folding station, "It's the pure version of ecstasy."

Kenzie said, "I've never bought drugs before. How would I, like, bring it up? Should I have cash on me when I ask? Or am I going to have to go to his house and hang out or something? He's the only person we know who deals. Well, my friend Kayla sells Adderall, but that's not *dealing* dealing. Anyway, my boyfriend's got his heart set on Molly. Have either of you ever bought drugs from Willis?" She straightened the maroon lacquered chair at the table in front of her.

Rhea said, "I wouldn't buy a homegrown tomato from Willis."

Byron sipped his coffee. "Willis doesn't sell Molly."

"Really?" Kenzie said. "Edgar told me he does. Shannon said so, too."

Byron said, "All Willis sells is meth. He calls it Molly, charges a premium, and dumb college kids don't know the difference."

Rhea cackled.

The door to Orsa's office opened with a groan, and Rhea shushed them. It was less about the drugs talk than the fact that sometimes Orsa took issue with what she deemed excessive socializing—if she heard chatter she assumed duties were being neglected.

Today, though, she didn't seem to be in a mood to scold but instead whistled to get the attention of all three, and gestured toward the table where Byron was already at work.

She pulled out chairs for Rhea and Kenzie and seated herself in the fourth.

"Can you guys keep something quiet?" When all three nodded, she proceeded: "There's a thief among us. One of your colleagues."

"Shit," Byron said. "Cash?"

Rhea said, "Liquor?"

"Rib eyes."

Kenzie made a face. "Oh my God, weird."

"What?" Rhea said. "Why?"

"If I knew the why," Orsa said, "I'd probably know the who. They took twenty-two and left two behind, in the walk-in."

"Danny discovered it this morning?" Rhea asked. "Doing inventory?"

Orsa nodded. "Somebody made off with them Saturday night I'm guessing, since nobody set foot in here between closing that night and Danny this morning. I'm trying to keep it quiet because I want to gauge honest first reactions. But I know it wasn't any of you guys."

Byron said, "How? I mean, obviously it wasn't, but."

"I just got done reviewing parking lot surveillance footage from the Wells Fargo," Orsa said. "It showed me everybody coming and going from noon Saturday through closing."

Rhea said, "Helpful?"

"Very. Ruled out over half the staff right away; everybody who left without a bag big enough to smuggle steaks is off the list. Between Danny, Larry, and me, we've searched this place top to bottom, nothing turned up. And twenty steaks is no small haul. Only a handful of staff come and go with a duffel or something big enough to handle that load. So, I've ruled out you two"—she nodded toward Kenzie and Byron—"since you carry that tiny purse, and you don't come with any bag at all. Rhea, from what I could tell, the bag you carry might technically be big enough. But you've been with me forever. I know your mother. Also, I know you aren't supposed to play favorites with your own kids, but you three are obviously mine, as you know."

Rhea said, "And we appreciate this."

Orsa continued, "Anyway, I already talked to Edgar and the Amish girl this morning and ruled them out, I just can't see it. And for that matter, they would've had to come back in later that evening and that would've shown up on the footage." Orsa tapped the yellow notepad in front of her, which displayed a handwritten list. "Here's my list of everybody who worked on Saturday and as you can see, I've crossed out everyone who left the restaurant without the means to transport. Which leaves only a select few. Chef Oz, for one, but I'm crossing him off because he's a chef, not an idiot; wouldn't go about it this way. So then the only others still on the list are Glen on the line, Shannon on pantry, Willis on dish, and Julia as host."

Rhea and Byron exchanged a look.

Kenzie said, "Say that again, you've narrowed it down to, who all? Glen, Shannon, Willis, Julia?"

Orsa referenced her list and nodded. "And let's keep our voices down; I know some of these people are clocked in already. Warn me if any of them are creeping up behind me."

"Glen's been with you longer than me," Rhea pointed

out. "He's been with you longer than anybody else. I'm just saying. If you're ruling people out on that basis."

Orsa flicked a crumb from the tablecloth. "Seniority is not the only consideration."

Byron said, "Leaving two steaks seems like some kind of message, doesn't it? There's no way that's an accident."

Kenzie added, "Especially with it being Grisham Day. Seems like sabotage."

"Agreed," Orsa said. "So since I've ruled out the three of you, I need you to be my eyes and ears. What do you think? Start with Glen. I know he's been with me forever, and Chef says he's solid on the line, but he's so quiet. I swear, sometimes weeks go by when he doesn't say a single word to me. He doesn't laugh at my jokes. He's about as much fun as a potato. Not like, well, Edgar, for instance."

"Aw," Kenzie said. "But I think Glen is just a nice, quiet man."

Rhea added, "And he really, actually cares."

"About the job?" Orsa clarified.

All three servers nodded.

Orsa said, "I know he doesn't show up late or make mistakes, but I'd need a little convincing that means he's some superstar or whatever you guys are trying to tell me. *He actually cares?* I don't know. Don't you all care?"

Rhea said, "A couple years ago, Glen saved up in order to buy his own set of knives so he wouldn't have to deal with the dull, scratched-up ones that get passed around. He transports his personal set every day. I think they're monogrammed with his initials."

Orsa made a face. "You say that like it's a good thing."

Kenzie said, "I think it's so cute. I think all old people are cute, I can't help it."

Rhea said, "He's not *old*, babe, just older than you. We all are."

"He's got more grays than me," Orsa said.

"Yeah, but you obviously—" Kenzie started. "Never mind."

"For what it's worth," Byron said, "as far as the steaks are concerned, Glen's a vegetarian nowadays anyway."

Orsa said, "Oh?"

Rhea nodded. "Ever since he started dating that lady who does the oils."

Orsa said, "He dates? Who? How?"

Kenzie said, "What do you mean *does the oils*?"

"Essential oils," Rhea explained to Kenzie. "I'm surprised she hasn't cornered you during your shiftie and tried to talk to you about hosting a party with your sorority pals."

"Huh? Why would anyone in my sorority want to buy oil?"

Rhea said, "Don't worry about it, babe."

Orsa waved her hands in the air. "Let's not get distracted. If it's not happening in my restaurant, I don't care."

Rhea said, "Well, since you put it that way and we're on the topic, you might as well know that apparently Glen's girlfriend brought a briefcase to the bar a while back. Darius told me, she was talking to other bar guests while she waited for Glen to finish up his shift."

"She held a sales meeting for her oils in my bar?" Orsa said.

Byron said, "The way I heard it, I don't think it was a

sales meeting, per se. She just had her stuff along in case anyone sitting at the bar happened to be interested."

"Still, that's about as tacky as it gets," said Orsa. "Should I ban her from the bar?"

Rhea said, "Anyhow, she's for animal rights and stuff, and Glen quit eating meat when they got together. Apparently she made him get rid of his snakes, too."

Byron nodded. "He asked me about taking a few of them in, when his girlfriend gave the ultimatum. He was desperate. Apparently rehoming a bunch of old snakes is not the easiest thing to do."

Kenzie said, "Did you?"

"God, no," Byron scoffed. "I don't know what he ended up doing about it. He was torn up. In love with his new girl, loyal to his old snakes."

"That's a good line," Rhea said. "You putting that one in your book?"

"What book?" Orsa said.

"Didn't you know Byron's a writer?" Rhea asked. "Taking his little notes in his little Moleskines day in, day out."

Orsa said, "But not a *writer* writer."

Kenzie announced cheerily, "He already said I can play myself as the dumb hot girl when the movie gets made."

Orsa waved her hands in the air again. "I don't care what you do in your free time. Actually, I do. But not right at this moment. So, we're leaning away from Glen? The vegetarian thing doesn't actually mean anything; he still could have taken them to, say, sell them. Or mess with me. We don't know that the thief stole them to eat them. I'm trying to get you guys to think outside the box. Is anybody mad at me? Glen doesn't ever seem mad. Just *there*.

What about the others? You guys are on the ground every day. Anybody doing more than the normal bitching and moaning?" She looked back down at her list. "Speaking of bitching and moaning, let's move on to Shannon. How's her attitude these days?"

The servers looked at one another. Rhea said, "It sucks, pretty much. She's fine. Awful lot of bitching and moaning though, like you said."

"About?"

"Oh, everyone. Edgar and Jane, for instance; that they didn't prep enough of this or that, didn't leave her good notes."

Orsa said, "We do run out of brûlées a lot, don't we? I keep seeing notes that we had to eighty-six mid-shift."

Byron pointed out, "That's not because Jane doesn't make enough, it's because Shannon ruins them with too much flame."

"Jesus. I'll have to talk to her about that waste." Orsa made a note next to her list of suspects. "The steaks, though. Shannon. What do we think? She's a single mom. Say she realizes the cupboards are bare, another week before payday. Mouths to feed. What do we think?"

Rhea said, "I don't think her kid has teeth yet."

Kenzie laughed.

Orsa said, "I think she still resents me is what I think, despite the fact I took her back after she had the kid and all. Not everybody would do that, you know, hold a spot. Most bosses don't want a pregnant moose huffing around or a weepy new mom in the workplace."

Kenzie said, "That *was* really nice of you, actually. I wouldn't expect you to hold my spot if I got knocked up then needed to take, what, like a couple months? I can't remember."

"Weeks," Orsa clarified. "But I'm glad you see it that way. I expected a little more appreciation from her, especially with the job market the way it is, but as soon as she returned she was right back at it with the nagging."

"Nagging?" Kenzie asked.

Orsa explained, "To move to front of house. It's not that she didn't make some efforts, trying to earn her way. But it's just one of those . . . Obviously, if you've met her . . . You guys get it. Can you imagine her on the floor? Interacting with guests? You guys get it."

Byron conceded, "We get it."

"Not everybody gets it, though. Shannon wouldn't drop it," Orsa reflected. "Not even after having the kid, when she ought to've been jumping for joy to have a job at all, she was right back at it, even pushier than before, saying how she needed to be making more, cost of raising a kid . . . Coming at me every time I saw her, about *when was I going to let her take the server test?*, begging to show me her wine presentation. Insisting she'd been studying the menu. It depressed me. And it's not like I'm against giving people opportunities. I'm all about that as a matter of fact—plenty of people consider me a mentor. Maybe you guys do. But it's got to make sense, got to be the right fit."

Byron said, "At least you got her off dish and on salads. That's a bump in pay, right?"

Orsa nodded. "I thought that would be the end of it but she still had her heart set on front of house. Got so bad for a while I avoided going in the kitchen when she was around. I know she was giving Rhea an earful about it for a while, too, *when am I gonna get my chance, can't you put in a word*, et cetera." Orsa glanced at Rhea who confirmed this with a nod.

Rhea turned to Kenzie. "It reached a fever pitch when you started training to serve."

"Me?" Kenzie said. "What've I got to do with it?"

"You'd been host for, what, a year or more, then when we lost Eli on the floor, that opened a serving spot and it made sense to train you to serve since you already knew the menu and table numbers. Which meant we needed to replace you as host."

"Ah," Kenzie said. "And you hired Julia to replace me, instead of giving Shannon a chance."

Rhea nodded. "Julia came on without any restaurant or really work experience at all. Couple years younger than Shannon, too, and a student, so probably not long term, whereas Shannon's likely here for the long haul, and—"

Orsa interrupted, "Are you really going to make me defend that decision? You agreed that when we moved Kenzie to the floor, Julia was the best candidate for new host."

Rhea said, "She was. I'm not saying it's not true. Just thinking how it would have looked to Shannon. And felt."

Kenzie said, "Well, I hope she was never mad at *me*."

Orsa said, "It's not like hosts make much more money anyway than Shannon does on pantry."

"A little more," Rhea clarified, "especially if you include their tip-out on a big weekend. But you're right, it's not *that* much more. I think it was more about the move to front of house, the trajectory. In back of house you hit the ceiling on the line, and nobody's ever replacing Glen as the lead there. Front of house, though, hosts and bussers usually become servers eventually, if they want to. Barbacks become bartenders. And servers and bartenders see way more money than anyone in the kitchen ever will."

"Really?" Kenzie said. "What about Chef Oz? I always figured he made more than everyone, even servers and bartenders. Do we make more than him? No wonder he's so snappy with us."

Orsa said, "Would you guys quit talking about how much money everybody makes? It's awkward."

Rhea said, "Chef snaps at us because he's a chef, good luck finding one that isn't a moody prick. You're just lucky you didn't have to work with the guy before."

Kenzie said, "So did Shannon eventually give up after Julia got hired?"

"I guess so," Orsa said. "The last time we talked about it, it's been ages now, I told Shannon that wine knowledge was the thing. Told her even if she had the menu memorized and could do the wine presentation and carry trays and all that, that the rest of you have extensive knowledge of wine. Regions, varietals, you're great with recommendations, you get the point. I guess that finally scared her off; I haven't heard boo about it in a while."

Kenzie said, "Wait, are we actually supposed to know that stuff about wine? I—"

Orsa cut in, "How'd we get onto this anyway? Steaks. So, Shannon's pissed about the Julia hire. Is she pissed enough to go the thieving route? I can see that. Can you guys see it?"

Byron shrugged. "I don't know Shannon well at all."

Rhea shook her head back and forth. "I don't know if I can see it. She's a little rough around the edges, but . . ."

Orsa said, "You're so good with words. That's why you're my manager. *Rough around the edges.*"

The kitchen door swung open, and Chef Oz entered the dining room.

Rhea said, "Greetings, Cosimo."

When he didn't respond, Rhea added, "Nice haircut," with a smirk. "You look fresh off the school bus."

"And you look day-old," Chef Oz said, wiping his brow into his shoulder. "Half off, I mean. If anybody's looking for a bargain."

Orsa said to the servers, "He already knows about the steaks. I talked to him when he got in an hour ago."

Chef Oz stood over the table with his tattooed arms crossed. "Are we gathered here for the big confession? Don't tell me . . . it was you," he pointed at Kenzie. "Mixer with the fraternity. Thought you'd win some points showing up with rib eyes instead of hot dogs."

Kenzie laughed.

"No?" Chef Oz turned to Byron. "It was you, wasn't it? You wanted a special treat for your only friend in the world, that ugly little mutt, your plus-one. Is it still alive? How old is that thing?"

"I don't actually know how old Ralphie is," Byron said, "seeing as he was a rescue. But thanks for the kind words, asshole. No wonder no one's ever rescued you."

Kenzie said, "I think anybody who gives a rescue a home is just like the best person."

Orsa said, "But you worry about the baggage."

Chef Oz turned to Rhea. "I know it wasn't you because you wouldn't have a clue what to do with a rib eye; you wouldn't know a proper mid-rare if it slapped you in the face." He turned to Orsa. "Did she tell you about the send-back Saturday?"

Orsa said, "I can't remember."

Rhea was nodding tiredly. "I tell you about all of them. This was the guy who said his mid-rare was a hair over, and he was right, so I had to insist on a refire."

Chef Oz clenched a fist and shook it at the air.

Orsa said, "I hate watching you guys fight. It pains me." To Chef Oz, she said, "Did you need something from me?"

"I did. Is Larry out picking up steaks right now?"

Orsa nodded. "Don't worry, I told him exactly what to look for, I know he's hopeless without specifics."

"I just wondered if he could grab a quart of cream and fresh mint too while he's out."

Orsa pulled out her phone and fired off a text.

Then she looked back down at the list of suspects and drummed her fingers on it. "What about Julia? She here yet?" She peered through the hall toward the host stand, which was around a corner and just out of sight, the tabletop lamp casting a golden arc of light.

Rhea looked at her watch. "She's probably in there now, returning voicemails. She usually comes at two thirty on Tuesdays—extra voicemails to return—unless I tell her otherwise."

"Can someone confirm?"

Chef Oz jogged down the hall that separated the bar from the dining room, returned, and confirmed: "She's here."

Orsa peered down the dark hallway. "I really can't fathom Julia," she mused. "But we've got to stick to the evidence. I need you guys to help get me to the finish line on this. Eyes and ears. Everything you know about everyone."

Rhea glanced soberly at Byron then tipped her head in Orsa's direction. "Are you going to tell her?"

"About what?" Byron said.

"Your conflict of interest."

Orsa looked back and forth between them. "Elaborate."

When Byron didn't speak up, Rhea said, "Byron and Julia are together. Right? Hooking up."

Byron muttered, "Oh God."

Orsa said, "Really, you and Julia?" She made a face. "But she's so pretty."

Chef Oz snorted laughter into his fist.

"It's intriguing, I mean," Orsa said.

"I concur," Chef Oz said with a little retch.

Kenzie said to Byron, "Well, I for one think you guys are so cute together."

"Thank you," Byron said, then turned to Rhea with a sour look. "And thank you for sharing my private business with the world. A courtesy I could always return, if you want me to." He raised his eyebrows.

Before Rhea could respond, Kenzie pointed out, "It can't be that private, though, Byron—you posted on Facebook about Julia just a few days ago."

Rhea said, "I didn't see that, I haven't been on recently. You and Julia are Facebook official?"

Kenzie jumped in to clarify, "No, they didn't change their relationship status, but he posted a cute picture of her at . . . where were you?"

Byron rolled his eyes. "We hiked Yellow Ridge last weekend. That overlook."

Chef Oz said, "Some guy died there a few years ago. His fiancée got him drunk and pushed him off the cliff. Julia probably had ambitions."

Orsa said, "We need to wrap this up. We didn't get to Willis, but I trust you'll tell me if you've got any compelling info." She turned to Byron. "And Rhea's right. You're off the investigation. It's a conflict of interest if you're screwing one of the suspects."

Kenzie screeched.

"What?" Orsa said. "I'm not allowed to say that word in my own restaurant? Don't be a prude." To Byron, she said, "You'd better not say a word to Julia until I've had my chance. Got it? No heads-ups."

"Got it," Byron said.

Orsa said to Chef Oz: "You haven't said anything to anyone other than us about the steaks, right?"

"Not a word."

Orsa turned to address all three servers. "Not a word, to anyone," she said again, pointing a finger at each of them for added emphasis. "I'm going to call in our remaining suspects for individual meetings when the time's right. Give them a chance to confess in my office, one-on-one." She straightened the large yellow gemstone pendant that hung at her neck.

Rhea said, "What's your plan if you get a confession?"

"I'll cross that bridge. I've got good intuition in the moment, when a kid needs the tough love route versus a path to redemption. I'll follow my heart." Orsa rapped her pen on the notepad and read the names aloud: "Glen. Shannon. Willis. Julia."

THE CHEF

OZ RETURNED TO THE KITCHEN AND SURVEYED his current company. Glen was wiping and stacking sauté pans fresh from dish. Shannon was counting desserts, her back turned. Her long, skinny neck swiveled as she bent and bowed and made notes on her whiteboard. Watching Shannon and contemplating the conversation that needed to happen, Oz stiffened with dread.

The silver lining to this steak business was that so far Orsa had been too distracted to bring up the newest Yelp reviews that had rolled in over the weekend. Half a dozen of them, all one and two stars. So-so on service. Brutal on the food. There had been a slew of bad ones in the past month. Oz didn't know if his palate was wrecked from picking up smoking again, or if the absence of inspiration was tangible, or if guests were getting more discerning or meaner, or what. It was concerning, even for someone who didn't give much of a shit. In any case, Oz was relieved that for the moment Orsa was too busy with her steak investigation to bring up the most recent reviews and start sticking spoons in his sauces. But this still left him with the terrible duty of warning Shannon.

Oz had gotten Shannon the job at Aunt O's several years ago after they had run into each other at the local dive bar. It was the first Oz had laid eyes on her in a decade and he never would have recognized her had she not approached and introduced herself. She was as tall as him. The bottom few inches of her light hair were dyed blue. Her face was covered in light and dark freckles. She was extremely interesting to look at, though far from beautiful.

They exchanged pleasantries and a few stories about Jeremy, Shannon's older brother and Oz's best friend since childhood, who was currently serving time for drugs and still a few years away from parole.

When they ran out of happy tales involving Jeremy, they caught up on their own lives.

Shannon was twenty-two, working in food service at a nursing home. She was still living with her mother in the same trailer where she and Jeremy were raised, in order to save enough money for college. She planned to become a veterinarian.

Oz said, "Ambitious."

"Is it?"

"For a twelve-year-old." He sipped his beer. "You're still a rug rat in my mind."

Oz was thirty, hired several years prior by Orsa whose last head chef, according to Orsa, was brilliant but had gone off the deep end. Before Aunt O's, Oz explained, he had cycled through many restaurant jobs and some catering.

Shannon gave Oz her number and asked him to give her a call if anything opened up at the restaurant. The nursing home was a drag, she said—she hated her boss there and was interested in working evenings and weekends anyway so that she could take on some part-time office work during the day.

Oz said, mostly joking, that they were currently looking for someone on dish since the last guy had threatened a server with a cheese grater.

He was surprised when Shannon jumped at the opportunity even after he warned her the dish pit was a hellscape of scalding water and harsh chemicals, abuse from cooks in need of pans and servers in need of glassware. They'd never had a girl on dish. Shannon said she could handle it, so Oz said okay because she actually seemed spirited enough to handle about anything, and of course because she was Jeremy's kid sister. And if Oz owed anyone a favor, or a thousand, it was Jeremy.

Oz's word went a long way with Orsa, who liked to sit in on interviews and have a say in hires but usually left the final decision to Oz or Rhea. Since Shannon had food service experience—she had even gotten her official Safe Serve certification—she was a shoo-in.

Oz hadn't expected that Shannon would start gunning for front of house so early, or at all. The rest of the back-of-housers had made their peace with their place. Willis in the dish pit, always reeking of weed, had teeth the color of cooked mushroom, and was probably a lifer. Glen, forty years old, man of few words, lover of reptiles, was definitely a lifer. Other cooks and dish guys Oz had worked with over the years were fresh out of rehab or high schoolers or gamers with incomprehensibly weak handshakes. None of them had any real ambition in the restaurant world and Oz hadn't guessed that Shannon would either. But after she overheard what the servers and bartenders pulled in on a busy weekend, there was no convincing her that it wasn't worth a try.

She asked Oz for advice about switching to front of house and he didn't have the heart to tell her it would not happen for her, for reasons that would hurt him to say aloud. So he told her to talk to Rhea and Orsa, explaining that the decision lay with them. Apparently neither of them had the heart to tell her it would never happen either, because for many months she continued to beg and try. She kept a menu and wine list at her salad station, studying during every bit of downtime. She cut the blue out of her hair. She learned the table numbers and advanced culinary terms. It was impossible to ignore her efforts. It was hard to watch.

They promoted her from dish to pantry (where she plated salads and desserts), which came with a small raise but did nothing to discourage her pursuit for front of house.

Then she got pregnant by her deadbeat boyfriend who left town before she was even starting to show and Orsa, sick of putting Shannon off a chance at front of house, came to Oz about the pregnancy, saying *now's our chance to let her go, and let her down easy.*

But because Shannon was Jeremy's kid sister, Oz couldn't let that happen. He gassed her up to Orsa, emphasizing how hard Shannon worked, how she was a perfectionist and an asset. He promised Orsa he would figure out the shifts Shannon would miss on account of the baby—he or Glen or Willis would cover salads and they would train servers on plating desserts in a pinch and they'd have Edgar overload on prep. The baby was due in the summer anyway, Oz pointed out; their slowest season. The prospect of working a skeleton crew and saving on labor during a slow time was appealing enough to Orsa that she agreed to hold Shannon's job.

Soon after Shannon's return, she brought up the front of house stuff again, with new targeted pleas about the cost of raising a child.

The Julia hire was a blow. When it circulated that Kenzie was going to train to serve, which would leave a vacancy at the host stand, Shannon got her hopes up, but instead Rhea and Orsa went with Julia, an outsider, an art history major with a fresh manicure and no work experience. Rhea and Oz commiserated privately about the Shannon issue and how the Julia hire would go over with her. But, they said, what could they do? *This was restaurant life; this was life.*

To be fair to Julia she was actually a great host. She hustled, she had a good attitude and sense of humor, she bussed and watered and filled in elsewhere as the need arose. But it was clear that Shannon would never forgive Julia for waltzing in to claim the front of house vacancy. There was little occasion for the two to interact but Shannon would create a skirmish over the dumbest infractions—where Julia set her ice water or how she arranged empty bottles in the recycling bin. Oz always tried to offer Julia a sympathetic expression to defuse the tension when Shannon's back was turned.

Over time, Shannon had gotten mouthier. She made

constant reference to the laziness of front-of-housers, how they loafed around even on a busy night, raking in the dough, while she and others in the kitchen busted their asses for half the take-home. She talked so much shit. She seemed to believe she was bulletproof in her current role, with Oz on her side. And Oz supposed she was; he would continue to champion her no matter how shitty her attitude got—and even if she was guilty of theft—because she was Jeremy's kid sister.

OZ AND JEREMY were best friends since early childhood, living in neighboring trailers and attending the same school. One day, Jeremy suggested that they slice their fingers to combine their blood and make the brotherhood official. Oz provided the Swiss Army knife.

As teenagers, they worked together at TGI Fridays, where Jeremy was on the fryer and Oz on dish. They drank milkshakes together at the end of the shift, compared burns and scrapes and stories from the rush, talked trash about everyone. Jeremy made passes at the bartenders who were old enough to be his mother and Oz laughed. Sometimes, they went to Randy the line cook's house for late nights, a known party spot. It was here that they fell in with a tough older crowd who operated in drugs—mostly meth—production, driving, dealing, using. Jeremy was quick-witted enough to make a good first impression; it took them longer to trust Oz. But eventually the two of them were offered the opportunity to get involved with the driving part. They were good candidates as young guys with jobs and cars and clean driving records.

Oz and Jeremy made a pledge to each other to never touch anything personally, not even a taste, except for booze and weed, and they stuck to that.

By the time they graduated high school they were making a lucrative trip every other weekend, from a drop spot outside of their town, to a middleman near Toledo. They'd meet the middleman along the highway and do the handoff inside a rest stop. On the drives, they'd eat beef jerky and listen to their favorite cassettes and alternate drivers. Whoever was off duty would drink a forty and count the cash and help watch for troopers.

As the hometown operation grew they were entrusted with more product and more frequent trips, and their earnings multiplied. They held onto the restaurant jobs for appearances, but turned down offers for promotions that would have meant increased responsibility.

The summer they both turned twenty-one, on one of their drives, a trooper's lights flicked on behind them.

It was a fluke that they were in Jeremy's car instead of Oz's that day. They both drove beaters but favored Oz's Corolla for these trips, because Jeremy's Escort was stick, Oz didn't know how, and the unspoken policy was that they spend roughly equal time behind the wheel.

But Oz had left his windows down for a rainstorm the previous night, the upholstery was soaked and stinking, so they were in the Escort today, with Jeremy at the wheel.

As the trooper got out of his car to approach, Jeremy said, "Oh, hell."

Unsteadily, Oz said, "Maybe just a taillight?"

The trooper claimed they'd been going five over, then claimed he smelled weed, which gave him probable cause.

He started to nose around, but before he'd gotten very far, he said, "Hang tight, boys," and turned back toward his car.

Oz thought perhaps they were in the clear, but Jeremy watched through the rearview window and said, "He's calling for backup. We're actually fucked."

It was silent inside the car for a bit. Oz felt sweat erupting everywhere, he felt immense pressure and itching on his skin. His head buzzed. He prayed.

Jeremy's voice reached him as a raspy whisper: "There's no reason for it to be both of us."

"Huh?"

They had joked about this possibility but never discussed it concretely. It seemed less likely to happen if a backup plan had never been articulated.

"It's my car," Jeremy continued. "And I'm at the wheel. There's no way I'm sliding. You've got a chance if we stick to a story. I'll say I brought you along unaware, you were just here for the ride, going to visit our buddy in the city. Just keep your mouth shut."

Oz shook his head vehemently. "But—"

"Don't let them nail us both. Just trust me. No matter what they say to you in the station. They'll try to play us against each other, try to get me to turn on you. I won't." Jeremy said. He paused, then added, "I know you'd do the same for me."

JEREMY TOOK THE full rap and kept his mouth shut even after they offered a reduced sentence should he testify to Oz's involvement. Oz knew the outcome would be bad but he wasn't expecting *nine years* bad, for a first trafficking offense. All those easy miles, the white powder tucked in the upholstery a vague and distant reality—it just hadn't seemed serious, at all.

Oz wept on the drive home from his first visit to the penitentiary, where Jeremy hadn't had much to say at all except to ask about his mom and his little sister, Shannon.

At TGI Fridays, Oz took the promotion from dish to salads that they had been offering him for ages. He excelled at that and was soon offered a spot on the line.

He found the adrenaline of the line during a busy shift to be a pleasant distraction from thoughts about Jeremy. The heat, the smells, the oil, the injuries, the music, the flow, the fights, the rush—it crowded out everything but the stress of the task before him. These were the only hours of the day that Oz was not assaulted by guilt.

Soon, Oz decided to take a second job and he landed at a sub shop that had a line out the door every day for lunch. Then he got in touch with the head of a local catering company and worked events for them when he could squeeze it in. The more Oz worked, the less he thought. The less free time he had, the fewer opportunities he had—and did not take advantage of—to visit Jeremy or reach out to schedule a call.

Oz heard about the opening at Aunt O's through industry word of mouth. The advertised pay was more than he made with all of his other jobs combined. He was also drawn to the prestige of the position. He didn't really think he'd be a legitimate candidate but studied up on the menu in advance of his interview anyway. He'd never set foot in the restaurant but had heard of it of course, as it was widely considered the nicest in town and very in demand for visiting parents.

He arrived at the interview in a collared shirt, armed with many compliments for Orsa's existing operation and a few ideas for higher-profit items he would add to the menu if she was interested—if not he'd be happy to just stick with the status quo and execute her recipes on the highest level possible. He said he knew she'd be taking a risk since he didn't come with a degree from culinary school nor with traditional fine dining experience.

Orsa said, sometimes risks worked out. "*Cosimo.*" She tapped his résumé. "Your mother Italian?"

Oz nodded. "More to the point, she enjoys a pink cocktail."

Orsa laughed. She asked about his tattoos.

It took him a few minutes of chitchat to realize that Orsa was flirting with him, sort of, so he flirted back, sort of.

Rhea sat in on the second half of the interview.

Orsa called to offer him the job half an hour after he walked out.

EVERYBODY AT THE restaurant loved Oz at first, when he was green and eager to please.

But the longer he was there, the meaner he got.

Nowadays, Oz was only as nice as was absolutely necessary in any given moment. He was just nice enough to

Orsa to keep his job, just nice enough to Rhea to operate harmoniously as managers of front and back of house. He was nice enough to Glen to keep him complacent because Glen was a beast on the line and if he left they'd be in a real bind. He was nice to Julia because he permitted himself one coworker crush at any given time. Unfortunately Byron had laid claim to Julia some time before, moving fast as he typically did. Not that Oz would have done anything about his crush even with Byron out of the picture—Julia was much too young and too sweet—but it did irritate him that she appeared to have fallen under Byron's tired tortured artist spell. And he was nice to Shannon because she was Shannon. That was it, everybody else could go to hell.

Oz knew he had turned into a proper asshole in his time at the restaurant. Whatever; whatever; oh well. Too bad. Chefs were assholes, it was a well-known hazard. But also, it wasn't quite that simple. Most chefs were assholes because they believed they deserved more than they were getting. More money, more respect, more creative license, more recognition, more help, more time off, more sleep, more sex, more attention, et cetera. It was the opposite for Oz. He was an asshole because he knew he deserved far less and far worse. He couldn't accept or enjoy the things he had—clean record, stable job, savings account—so, in fact, the more he gained, the more he lived, the more miserable he had become. And he found creative ways to torture himself even further, such as developing crushes on coworkers who were out of his league, routinely sleeping fewer than five hours a night, and refusing medication or to lift with his legs despite persistent back pain.

The things that separated Oz's and Jeremy's lives now were impossible for Oz to hold in his head in a meaningful or sustained way. The set of circumstances that had placed them in Jeremy's car that day instead of Oz's were so minute and so meaningless that any tiny twist of fate could have changed everything. Sheer, random chance that they were in Jeremy's vehicle. That was one way of looking at it; the other way was nothing to do with chance. The other truth was that there was a gaping abyss between the two men involved: a good one, a bad one.

How could Oz see it any way but that way?

In his darkest moments Oz allowed himself to touch the truth: That when Jeremy said, *You'd do the same for me*, he was dead wrong.

GLEN WAS IN his own world and the music was loud, so Oz sidled up next to Shannon at her station moments after reentering the kitchen.

She jumped. "Whoa there," she said. "Careful, I've got this knife."

"Keep doing what you're doing," Oz whispered. "Don't look at me. Orsa knows."

"What?"

"Shh," he said. "Keep looking straight ahead and get back to your chopping. Careful, that spot on the pepper. Keep your head down. I don't want her to see us talking."

"Why?"

"She's about to come in with questions," Oz whispered. "She knows about the steaks. And she's already got it narrowed down to just a few people. She's going to come looking, asking, or she might not say anything but head straight down to snoop in lockers. Here's the plan: You stay right here, be cool, don't move from your station. Be ready to play dumb. I'm gonna head downstairs right now, grab your cooler from your locker and run it out. I'll stash it in my car til the end of the shift."

"What are you talking about?" Shannon said.

"The missing steaks," Oz hissed. "She knows it was you." He paused. "That neoprene cooler you keep in your locker. I know you wouldn't have Saturday's steaks in there still, but I assume you've got some other work food stashed in there, like usual, and we need to get it out of the restaurant before she starts snooping. If she finds any restaurant food in there at all, she'll take it as proof the steaks were you, too." Shannon regarded him quizzically and alarms started to fire off in his head. He murmured, "Isn't it... You always have it... I assumed..."

"I'm sorry," Shannon said, setting down her knife and turning to look at him. "You think I'm stealing food?"

Oz's thoughts scrambled hopelessly. He hadn't even considered the possibility he was wrong. Shannon was supposed to be thanking him right now, as he was supposed to be saving her.

"You think I'm stealing?" she repeated. "Hiding food in the cooler in my locker?" She barked out a laugh.

Oz attempted feebly to walk back the accusation. "I just assumed with that cooler you always haul around but keep out of sight... I figured you were taking little bits of this or that... Never enough to amount to anything or register on inventory but you know, enough to keep you fed at no cost... So the steaks that disappeared Saturday,

I just thought, because you're always complaining about money . . . I guess I thought you were struggling."

Shannon stared at him. "I *am* struggling."

"Shit, dude. Sorry." Oz paused. "So then, what's with the cooler?"

Shannon snorted. "It's my *milk*, you moron."

"Milk?"

"I pump in the bathroom once or twice every night. I always try to go home with a couple ounces."

Hot blood filled Oz's cheeks. "Why didn't you ever say anything? I would've covered you for longer breaks or more of them."

"Because you guys are all so weird about stuff like this. Not to mention, the last thing I need is Orsa thinking I'm sneaking off and taking extra breaks, taking extra liberties now that I've got a kid." She laughed. "Dude, I can't believe you thought I was stealing little nibbles like some rat. You know I hate the food here. I can't believe you thought . . ." She shook her head and laughed again. "Wait." She paused. "You said some steaks went missing? Orsa's narrowed it down and I'm on the short list? You thought it was me because of the cooler. Is she onto the cooler thing too? Am I going to have to explain to Orsa about the pumping?"

Oz shook his head. "I don't think she has any strong reason to suspect you personally, except she thinks you're still bitter about the Julia hire."

"She's right."

"More so, I think it's that she's ruled out almost everybody else for one reason or another. So, listen. Forget I said anything. Just give her straight answers and you'll be fine."

"I swear, if she accuses me . . . If somehow I end up losing my job over this . . ." Shannon's voice rose.

"You won't," Oz assured her. "As long as you keep your cool, you'll be fine. She's going to find the actual thief."

"She'd better," Shannon said. She was quiet for a moment, looked over her shoulder and back into the rest of the kitchen where Glen was no longer at his station. "You know what? Screw this," Shannon said. "I'm gonna go talk to her right now."

"Please don't," Oz said. "I swore I wouldn't give anyone a heads-up."

"I won't throw you under the bus," Shannon said. "But I'm also not gonna play dead for the next two hours while she conducts her little investigation."

"I think that's exactly what you should do," Oz said.

"Too bad. Glen's not at his station—she's probably giving him the shakedown right now."

"Glen can handle himself," Oz said. "Just wait your turn."

"Nah," she said. "I'm gonna go say my piece. Glen can handle himself but can he defend himself? Besides, what's the worst that could happen?"

"You lose your temper and say something bad enough to get yourself fired."

"I'm a grown woman," Shannon said.

"Suit yourself. Seriously though, watch your mouth if you want to keep your job. She's in a mood, even for her."

"Noted."

Oz left Shannon's side and made his way back to the stove, where his butternut squash soup simmered in the large kettle stockpot. He examined it while in his peripheral vision Shannon was vigorously finishing up her chopping.

The color of the soup was somewhere between tangerine and peach, the texture smooth and properly thickened. Oz dipped a spoon and blew on it until it no longer steamed. He swished it around his mouth and swallowed, tapped his tongue on the roof of his mouth and took some nasal inhales to pull the full palate. The coconut came through, the onion came through, the cinnamon and cayenne were there on the finish, but the tartness from the granny smith apple was nowhere to be found. He had used the last of the apples and it wasn't worth anyone's time to run out for more—he'd just hit it with a tiny bit of red wine vinegar for acidity, and a pinch or two more salt would help too.

He heard Shannon leave the kitchen and considered the information he had acquired. In light of this, he tried to formulate a new theory about the theft—a different culprit—and found himself unable. If it wasn't Shannon, then according to Orsa's list that left only Glen, Willis, and Julia. Glen, with his loyalty and his monogrammed knives? Willis, who only held down a job to serve as a legitimate source of income on paper, when he made twice as much selling drugs? Julia, with her smile, her leather jacket, and her bright future? Oz was relieved on the one hand that Shannon was innocent, disappointed on the other that he was denied the opportunity to help her, and genuinely baffled by the prospect that any of these three remaining suspects were the guilty party.

Oz wrestled briefly with a hazardous notion that perhaps Orsa had taken the steaks herself, concocting the whole scheme as an excuse to confront Shannon and inspire a meltdown that would result in Shannon walking out. In that case, he thought, Orsa might have "confided" in Oz and the servers merely for appearances, or to take their temperature. This sort of plan seemed not exactly beneath Orsa, but also unnecessarily risky and elaborate.

Then Oz considered another unpleasant possibility: that Shannon would relay this scenario—Oz's assumption of her guilt—to Jeremy the next time they spoke.

Jeremy's name didn't come up often anymore between Shannon and Oz, but Oz was aware that either Shannon or her mom still went for visits to the penitentiary every couple weeks, whereas Oz's last had been over a year ago. He'd had such a terrible feeling on that visit, about the look in Jeremy's eyes. It was either love or it was hate.

Several months into his job at Aunt O's, and once Oz had actually gotten to know Rhea, she confided in him that Orsa hadn't actually hired him because he was the best candidate for the job; far from it. Rhea said that Orsa had selected Oz because she wanted to go with someone malleable, who wouldn't put up any resistance to doing things her way. The last chef, Luca, a bullheaded diva, had been such a pain in her ass. According to Rhea, "a manageable man" were Orsa's exact words about Oz.

Oz said to Rhea, "I really wish you hadn't told me that."

Orsa was wrong, of course. Manageable or not, Oz knew, he was no man.

THE LEAD LINE COOK

GLEN WAS ASSEMBLING INGREDIENTS FOR chimichurri when Orsa entered the kitchen and whistled like a coach. Glen glanced around to confirm her intended audience. Chef Oz was standing with Shannon at her station at the far end of the kitchen and there was no one else in there, so it had to be him.

He followed Orsa from the kitchen and through the dining room where the servers were scattered on side work. Down the hall she opened the door to her office.

Only once in his seven years at the restaurant had Glen been summoned to Orsa's office spontaneously like this, and the memory of that conversation produced a jolt of optimism—it was when he had been promoted from fry cook to lead line cook, which came with a small raise. Although a promotion was out of the question since now he was second only to Chef Oz, there had been recent whispers that Orsa was batting around the idea of a health plan she would offer to full-timers such as Glen. He thought now, with a swell of hope, *That must be it.*

Glen had been without health insurance for his entire adult life. He'd survived all sorts of fevers and aches and dental calamities. And while he was certain, given his history of survival, that he would survive anything else, too, either a health plan or a raise that would make the occasional doctor's visit affordable would provide immense relief.

In her office, Orsa nodded toward the chair that faced her desk and when she closed the door behind Glen, he was all but certain good news was on the way. He needed good news today. Any sort of a break or a boost or even just a meaningless gesture.

Orsa took a seat and gave him an appraising look before she spoke.

Glen wiped his hands on his apron and crossed his legs.

Eventually she spoke, unpleasantly. "Anything you want to say to me?"

Glen thought. "No?"

Orsa raised an eyebrow and leaned. "Sure about that?"

Deflated, Glen's mind ticked through possibilities aside from good news that would necessitate a private conversation. Had he messed something up over the weekend? Lost a hair into a stew pot? He was so careful. And Orsa usually preferred to issue a scolding when she had a bigger audience.

Orsa exhaled through her nose. "Somebody stole a bunch of meat Saturday. I'm not saying it was you. I'm saying if it *was* you, and you fessed up here with me now, I'd be more lenient—discreet, even, probably—than if I have to find out on my own." Her eyes were bleary and enormous behind her reading glasses.

Glen was stunned by both the theft and the accusation.

Orsa seemed to register his surprise and in a softer tone she added, "You've been with me a long time. Like I said, I'm not saying it was you. I just like to face things head-on. I pride myself on direct communication. I think we all have room to grow there."

Before Glen could respond, the door behind him burst open and Shannon was there, huffing in a berry-stained apron, sweat beading across her brow.

Orsa said, "Excuse me, Missy, how about a knock? Christ Almighty."

Shannon closed the door behind her and moved forward to stand at Glen's side. "Couldn't help but overhear," she said. "Steaks gone missing?"

"Wow," Orsa clicked her teeth together. "And eavesdropping."

Shannon said, "Who all have you called into your office about this, trying to coerce a confession? Who else have you pulled in, aside from Glen?"

"I'm just getting started," Orsa said. "You're next on the list."

Shannon said, "How lovely of you, starting your inquisition with your lowest-paid employees. Oh, and Willis; I assume he's on your list there, too, as soon as he gets in."

Orsa said, "You know what everybody gets paid, do you?"

"We all know what we all get paid. Only rich people are weird about money."

"I have my reasons for talking to the people I'm talking to."

Shannon said, "You're out of your mind if you think Glen would steal a crouton, much less a bunch of steaks."

Orsa glanced at Glen then back to Shannon. "That may be true. But since you're here now, too, let's go ahead and just get it all on the table. Pull over that chair."

Shannon's fists were dug into her hips. "I'd prefer to stand."

Orsa said, "I don't like you looming over me like a T-Rex. Get that chair."

Shannon did so with a grunt and took a seat next to Glen.

Orsa said to Shannon, "Here I am, trying to get to the bottom of this steak business. And here you come, busting in on a private meeting with that tone." Orsa situated herself higher in her chair. "We've had our issues, but this is another level, disrespect-wise. Some might say that's just cause for termination."

"Oh, you're going to fire me now?" Shannon squawked. "Because I don't take kindly to a false accu—"

"Actually, there's something else," Orsa interrupted. "Forget the steaks. Apparently, you've been burning brûlées."

Shannon's mouth dropped open.

"The Yelp reviews of late," Orsa added.

"We've been through this already! Every time one of these reviews pops up, you're in my ear about it."

Orsa said, "Just wanted to mention it again. Get you to ponder the *waste*." She turned to Glen. "The steaks weren't my only business with you either. There's something else with you too that the servers were telling me about."

Glen felt like he was underwater and flailing. The Yelp

reviews, even the bad ones, almost never mentioned an item he was responsible for.

Orsa said, "I heard that your girlfriend is conducting sales meetings in our bar. The word is, she's bringing in a bunch of oils, whipping them out while she waits for you to finish your shift. Maybe it was just the once. Anyway, it's inappropriate. Possibly even illegal, I'd have to ask Larry, without a permit or—"

"Dude." Shannon was practically frothing at the mouth. "You are unbelievable! You—"

"Doesn't involve you," Orsa snapped. "You can see yourself out any time."

Shannon said, "You think it's a good idea to go down this route today, of all days? What if me and Glen decided we're done with your bullshit and walked out right now? Good luck getting dinner on the table for John Grisham without—"

"*You* think," Orsa cut in, "it's a good idea to come in here raising your voice at your boss in this job market?" Orsa held up a finger to Shannon and turned back to Glen. "I wasn't finished with you," she said, her tone suddenly genial. "Glen. My point was, about the oil thing, that I'm willing to forget about it and not say anything to your girlfriend or have her banned or anything like that."

Glen said, "Actually—"

"In fact," Orsa continued, "what I really wanted to say if Shannon hadn't interrupted is that if your girlfriend wants to conduct her business here, she's welcome to. How about that? I just need to double-check that it's not illegal; that's the only reason I brought it up. And in that case, she can have a high-top all to herself—room to spread out. How's that?" She directed her gaze at Shannon. "And you act like I'm so stingy." She settled back further into her chair and a blast of her musky and floral perfume reached Glen. "What do you think? What do you say?"

Glen was struggling with both the thinking and the saying. It was an ongoing problem.

The origin story of this ongoing problem was either a long story or a very short one, depending how you looked at it. Also, depending how you looked at it, it was either a triumph or a tragedy; the ending either happy or sad or yet to be determined.

ON A SNOWY day when he was eight years old, Glen let his mutt, Ramses, out into fresh snow without his leash. Ramses was a sweet but psychotic sheepdog mix. He couldn't be trusted off leash, yet the dog's exuberance for the snow thrilled Glen to distraction. He watched Ramses hop through the deep and drifted snow. Glen threw snowballs, and Ramses lunged.

Glen saw the rabbit before Ramses did and realizing what could happen, Glen tried to get to the dog in time, hollering and offering treats and running his way. But before Glen had gotten close enough to grab hold of his collar, Ramses spotted the rabbit. The large, dark cottontail stared at Ramses and hopped once, perfectly vertical like a dare, then it took off.

The rabbit bounded graceful as a gazelle, Ramses barreled after it, Glen after Ramses.

Glen panted through the snow, screaming for the dog, as the rabbit zigged and zagged.

Over the train tracks and past the Sunoco then through, then past, the Graystone trailer park. There were moments where Ramses was out of his view. Although he couldn't keep pace with the dog who couldn't keep pace with the rabbit, there were the tracks in the snow to follow.

Just beyond the residential outskirts, the rabbit beelined for Black Creek Forest, a small but thickly wooded area. The forest was private property without any homes built within it, owned and used instead by hunters. Faded purple No Trespassing signs had been posted along the trees at its border for as long as Glen could remember and he had always respected them. But when the dog hurtled past the No Trespassing signs and into the dense woods where no trails were discernible under drifted snow, Glen's loyalty blinded him to any consideration of his own safety.

And in any case, he was not far from his home, a mile or two at most.

But once Glen was in the woods, everything changed. He lost sight of Ramses and the rabbit almost immediately. Then an icy, swirling gust of wind came surging through and stole their tracks from the snow right before him. Glen put his hands to his mouth, cupped and screamed: "Ramses!" He spun and spun to send his voice in every direction.

He spun until he was disoriented. The wind twisted and billowed over the snowy landscape once again, swallowing his own tracks. He turned around. Thick evergreens seemed to have converged to conceal the path back out behind him. He had no idea which way was which.

He screamed, "Ramses! Come back to me!" into the woods and ran frantically in one direction then another, zigging and zagging like the rabbit had done. When he stopped running, he shivered and wept. “Come back to me!” he pleaded into the woods.

Then he ran more.

Then it began to snow.

That was the last thing he could recall of the event—the falling of fresh snow.

But evidently after some time had passed, he found his way to a backyard that bordered the east end of the woods, where he was discovered by a family who saved his life.

He spent a long time in the hospital. Dehydration and hypothermia, related complications, including brain damage.

They said he was lucky to be alive. They said there was no way to gauge the long-term implications of the damage, which could fade or resolve or worsen incrementally or sporadically. They stressed that he was lucky to be alive.

Miracle was the word his mother used again and again to describe his survival, suggesting he could consider it a point of pride.

Lucky and miraculous as he may have been, when Glen returned to school he found that no one would meet his eyes. No one seemed to know what to say.

So any pride he might have felt—from his mother's influence and at the fact of his survival—faded with time when day after day he found himself alone and eventually he had no conclusion to draw but that there was some part of it all for which he should feel shame.

Confusing matters further was the fact that it was impossible for Glen to gauge accurately the nature and extent of cognitive change in himself. Long swaths of time before the incident were murky and amorphous in his memory, devoid of certainty. He couldn't really remember if he'd had friends before but if so it seemed he no longer did. Sometimes the word for extremely common objects eluded him. He rarely understood the basis of jokes. He was mystified by body language and subtleties in communication. His academic difficulties mounted. He tried so hard. But so often he could not remember what he needed to know. These problems coupled by the feeling of rejection caused Glen to retreat even further, losing confidence in his ability to speak and eventually falling almost altogether silent.

WHEN HE WAS sixteen Glen decided he must look for work to fill his evenings and weekends because his mother was having a hard time providing. He knew he would struggle with the interview process and certain skills in any workplace but hoped a strong head-to-the-ground work ethic might be enough.

The Burger King that was walking distance from his home had recently updated their huge swinger sign out front to advertise NOW HIRING! status—where for several months prior, the sign had instead advertised: EAT HERE AND DI E LIKE A KING!

Glen decided to apply. Despite his lack of experience and difficulty making eye contact during the interview, he was offered the position.

The hiring manager, a bony woman with a wide mouth, explained, "It's me and my sisters run this place, pretty much. We just need somebody on fryer who can take the heat and doesn't talk much. Minnie did it for a while, but she slipped on grease and dislocated her knee.

You're gonna need nonslip shoes, by the way. Payless's got the best selection for the best price. Anyway, Barb's been on fryer since Minnie's fall and she does okay but she can't keep up with the weekend volume. She bitches nonstop about the heat, and nobody wants to listen to her yapping."

Glen thought she might be exaggerating but after a few shifts, he came to realize the entire place was literally staffed by the same family—the manager, her six sisters (among them, two sets of twins), and a handful of cousins. The sisters fought constantly but ran an efficient operation from what Glen could tell, with firmly established roles and expectations.

Glen came to enjoy his job much more than school. Aside from opening and closing and stocking duties, he spent all day over the fryer—monitoring temps, keeping the basket and oil as clean as possible, packing and dipping and timing the frying of french fries, onion rings, and chicken nuggets. It played to his strengths with straightforward and repetitive tasks that required little interaction with coworkers aside from occasional clarifications and special requests, and none whatsoever with guests. The stench of grease permeated his clothing and his hair. The heat could be oppressive, and occasionally he suffered a burn. His feet and wrists were often cramped painfully by the end of a shift. The incessant yelling of the sisters gave rise to low-grade anxiety even though it was rarely directed at him. But the paychecks brought him pride, and his mother peace of mind.

He had been at Burger King for a year when a horde of cops showed up mid-shift one day and ordered everyone out of the building. One of the sisters took off on foot and a cop took off after her.

A few days later, the local paper detailed the indictments: fraud, embezzlement, drug trafficking. Glen was the only person on staff who wasn't named. His mother read the article with great interest. She said she didn't think it would hurt his future job opportunities, and sure enough, he was able to secure a job at Wendy's soon after.

He worked at Wendy's on fryer, uneventfully over the course of his final years of high school, and for some years past graduating.

When his manager at Wendy's took a job at Applebee's and asked Glen if he'd be interested in joining her there for a small raise and more favorable conditions, Glen was floored and happy to accept. The fry station at Applebee's was more complex, with mozzarella sticks and crispy cheese curds and wontons and chicken wings, the overall volume was higher than at Burger King or Wendy's, the dinner rush more intense. But with time Glen developed and mastered his own system. The chef took notice and trained Glen up on salads and desserts, too, so that he could fill in there. Glen did so well and was so reliable that the chef eventually decided he wanted Glen as his right-hand guy on the line. Glen worked at Applebee's for many years until out of nowhere corporate announced that the location would close. They were no longer profitable. There were a variety of factors, including supply chain issues, new liability requirements and new competition in a town where Applebee's had once been the best option for visiting university parents. *Skanky faux-Italian* was how the franchise owner bitterly characterized one of these new restaurants, the only one billing itself "fine dining."

Within weeks of Applebee's closing down, Glen responded to an ad for a cook at the skanky faux-Italian establishment.

He was interviewed by the owner, Orsa, and Chef Luca, an intense, red-faced man who informed Glen that he was being interviewed based on stellar references from former managers and the Applebee's chef.

Chef Luca said, "They all said you wouldn't say much in the interview, but I'd be a fucking idiot not to hire you. So what am I gonna do? Make some kinda fucking idiot out of myself?" He stared at Glen. "Do you think I'm the kinda guy that's gonna make some kinda idiot out of himself?"

Glen said, "No, sir."

Glen worked peacefully enough under Chef Luca, having been conditioned to workplace tempers long ago by the Burger King sisters but he was nevertheless relieved when Chef Luca was replaced by Chef Oz, who had a softer tone.

And Chef Oz was good to Glen, putting faith in him, increasing his duties to include more side and soup prep, butchering, freezer and pantry organization, all of which Glen enjoyed.

The decades-long journey from fast food to sit-down to fine dining, and from fryer to lead line cook, had been tremendously gratifying to Glen.

Crucially, Glen's cognitive challenges did not draw attention in this field. At worst, he might be accused now and then of not speaking loudly or enough. But he executed. He never came late. He never left a task undone. Even as lead line cook Glen still didn't make enough money at Aunt O's to take a vacation or replace his shitty car or move from his shitty one-bedroom rental to anything larger or less shitty, but he did not entertain a social life anyway and so was not pained by a modest lifestyle. He took genuine daily pride and pleasure in his work.

WORKING THE LINE was one thing, though, and meetings with management were quite another.

Things here in Orsa's office were becoming more muddled by the second.

Glen couldn't remember why Shannon was in the room with him and Orsa, he couldn't follow about these missing steaks and his role in any of it. He couldn't understand why he was embroiled in conflict at all when he just wanted to go wipe down his station so that everything would be ready and perfect for John Grisham.

Orsa and Shannon both seemed to be awaiting a reaction and Orsa prompted him: "Your girlfriend? The oils?"

"Oh," Glen said. "She quit the oil thing a while ago. And anyway, she's not my girlfriend anymore."

"Oh," Orsa said. "Really? As of when?"

"Recently."

"I'm sorry. The servers didn't tell me."

"I didn't tell them."

Shannon faced him. "Shit, Glen, I'm sorry. It seemed like you were getting serious."

"I'm sorry too," Orsa said. "Find the bright side, though. Are you allowed to eat meat again? I'm sorry, I shouldn't make light. I'd offer you a couple shots of Jack and a box of Kleenex if it wasn't Grisham Day."

Shannon said, "Are you going to get your snakes back?"

Misery and humiliation clobbered Glen's heart and although he hadn't yet spoken a harsh word, not at Jade, not even *about* her, the longer she remained a topic of conversation, the closer he felt to an outburst of some kind.

The story of their relationship was stupid, and that was the worst part of it—its stupidity. Glen's stupidity, laid bare. It was the sort of story that people wouldn't be able to repeat without a chuckle at his expense.

GLEN HAD MET Jade the year before, at the library. He was there because he had dropped his phone in a toilet and wouldn't have money to replace it for several months. He went to the library to check his email and bank account and the forecast. Jade was on her way out as he was on his way in and she was juggling a huge stack—everything from carrot farming to haikus to embalming—which she dropped. Glen was nearby and helped her reassemble her pile. He commented on her tattoos, not as an advance but with genuine interest, and she suggested a coffee.

A week later, she read his palms and proclaimed the two of them soulmates.

Glen hadn't ever had a girlfriend. Not even close. Instead, in the years since adolescence, outside of his restaurant jobs, all that had occupied him were the four pet snakes he had acquired—pets that would not mind his long shifts—and the tomatoes he grew in his window wells.

Where women were concerned, he might occasionally admire from afar the attractive girls who worked at the restaurant, but did not harbor any inclination to flirt, much less develop a lasting crush.

But then Jade came along, sweeping Glen up with the velocity of a tornado. She was only a few years younger than Glen but had the energy and twinkling eyes of a teenager. She loved art and adventure and had lived in a dozen countries, although to hear her talk about that, it sort of sounded like homelessness.

She said that Glen was unlike any man she had ever met before. She didn't mind that he didn't talk much. She explained that that made him the yin to her yang.

Soon, she moved out of the rented farmhouse she shared with six roommates and into the rental Glen shared with his snakes. She said, "Why snakes?" He said because he had lost the only other pet he'd ever had, a beloved childhood dog, and couldn't bear the thought of a pet that couldn't live contentedly in confinement.

He said there was no need for her to contribute to household expenses—he'd been handling things on his own for a long time. She said she would be grateful to focus on herself and would pitch in monetarily whenever she settled into something.

It wasn't that she lacked ambition or interests. She had all kinds of those. She made jewelry. She did open mics. She created chapbooks and sold them out of her car. She dyed people's hair. The oil thing. A similar thing, with organic powdered smoothies. Some dog-walking, some dried flower arrangements. None of her projects amounted to enough income that she was able to contribute meaningfully toward rent or groceries, but she did some cleaning around the house, and she ushered Glen into a new way of living.

With Jade, Glen's home was filled with music and candlelight, talk of spirits and souls. Jade was so convincing in her certainty of their shared destiny that Glen did not question it. She described visions and symbols, recited poems about true love, read tarot, looked deep into his eyes. She spoke of the path of surrender, the dissolving of one's self. When Glen had headaches or a sore back, Jade did incantations and massaged special concoctions into his scalp or love handles. When he could recall a dream, she could inform him on its meaning.

All of this amazed Glen, who had never before in his life read a poem voluntarily nor focused on his breath. Now, every day, he felt himself changing, changing, changing.

There was the small trouble of money. Glen's budget was already tight before Jade moved in and with the increased cost of groceries for two and the occasional splurge, the budget went from tight to untenable. He didn't want her to feel his stress where money was concerned so instead of having a conversation about it, he cut back on his own expenditures. He switched phone plans. He skipped oil changes. He sold a watch of his grandfather's that he never wore anyway because it was impractical. None of this was anything more than small trouble.

The only big trouble, where Jade was concerned, was the snakes.

Well, not the snakes, exactly. Jade didn't object to Glen's keeping reptiles as pets once she was assured of their comfort, animal lover that she was. She was, however, horrified when she learned about the feeding practice of live mice dropped into their cages twice a week.

The first time she was present for a feeding, it was a whole thing—she screamed and wouldn't stop screaming.

When she calmed down, Glen pointed out that she didn't have to watch. But she was adamant the practice not continue, and he said, *Okay, okay.*

Glen baked her a vegan apple crisp that evening to smooth things over and she was appreciative.

In the coming weeks, Glen exhausted all sorts of options for other methods of feeding, but the snakes refused to eat anything aside from the live rodents to which they'd grown accustomed. When the mice were discontinued, the snakes went on full hunger strike.

As the snakes grew listless and weak, Glen started buying mice on the sly and feeding them to the snakes when Jade was out of the house. He hated to keep a secret but couldn't see a way around it. This worked fine for a while until one day she caught him in the act.

Jade went ballistic. Glen begged forgiveness. She almost left. She dangled one foot out the front door.

In the heat of the moment, Glen said he would do anything, *anything*, to make her stay, and she replied it was either her or the snakes. She said she respected the snakes' autonomy but could not tolerate the ritualistic torture of mice, under her roof. Given that Glen had failed to establish any other way to keep the snakes fed, Jade said the only solution to this problem was for him to get rid of them. As for an ethical rehoming, instead of releasing the snakes to the wild or contacting an agency that might eventually euthanize them, Jade suggested Craigslist.

In hindsight Glen realized there were glaring faults in Jade's logic and not just about this snake business. But at the time, his determination to save his relationship, to keep the peace with his soulmate, eclipsed all other considerations. He acquiesced to her demands and posted on Craigslist, advertising his beloved snakes and all the related equipment at a fair price. When he did not get any inquiries, he lowered the asking price incrementally until eventually he was advertising them at no cost whatsoever for anyone who could promise a proper and loving home.

He got a few inquiries once the whole setup was free and within days a man who went by Birch came to pick up the entire haul, in a mint green pickup truck. Glen wanted to ask if he could come visit his snakes sometime but thought that might be weird, so instead he asked if Birch would be willing to send a few pictures from time to time, and Birch said, *You got it, brother.*

But an hour later, when Glen called the number Birch had provided, to tell him he had left behind one of the heat lamps, he was informed that Birch's number was out of service.

Birch did not respond to any of the messages Glen sent in the coming days, and his Craigslist profile disappeared. Glen thought about contacting Craigslist, but didn't know what exactly to report.

Jade was unsympathetic to Glen's distress.

"What are you worried about?" she said. "No one would take in a snake that didn't want a snake."

It took Glen a while to let it go, to stop mulling over the unknown fate of his snakes. But he did eventually let it go, and things were normal with Jade for a while again. Glen was so relieved to be past their first real conflict. He baked another vegan apple crisp.

Then just last week Jade left with one of her old roommates to attend a music festival in Ohio. She did things like this now and then. But this time she was gone for two days longer than anticipated, and when she came home on Sunday morning she said she had fallen in love with a magician. "I know it sounds cliché," she said, "but it really was magical."

She told Glen she would be packing her things and heading to Sandusky that very evening, where the magician was waiting for her.

She delivered all of this information with little emotion and when she had wrapped up, she shrugged helplessly. "I know it's not what either of us expected," she said. "We've had a beautiful journey together, Glen. But I need to surrender to the universe on this."

Glen was confused. He said, "You said we were soulmates."

"A person can have more than one," Jade explained. She gave him a sad look. "Haven't I taught you anything?"

Within a few hours, she was gone.

Two days later and back at work, Glen was still in shock, really. It wasn't just that Jade was gone. It was everything she had given and taken, everything she had changed. It was how quickly the world had gone from a place where Glen had not only a soul but a soulmate, to a world where nothing—not one thing—was sacred; a world where snakes could vanish and all you'd have were your memories and the memories of your dreams, and maybe a few shriveled-up, discarded skins.

GLEN HAD NO idea what he'd missed in this meeting with Orsa and Shannon while his thoughts had meandered to Jade.

"I'm dead serious," Shannon was saying to Orsa. "If me and Glen walk out right now, you're screwed tonight."

"Is that a threat?" Orsa said. "Don't worry. You leave if you want to leave. We'll be just fine."

"Oh, are *you* gonna hop on salads?" Shannon demanded, with a laugh.

"I'll call Edgar back in, watch me," Orsa said. "He loves me. Look, I'm sending him a text right now. He'll come back in and cover whoever I need him to. Just watch."

"Fat chance," Shannon said. "Edgar never answers his phone once he's clocked out. *Never.* And if he did, I'd love to see him survive five minutes on the line under actual pressure."

Glen was lost in his head again, assaulted by images and ideas that did not relate to the matter at hand.

JADE WAS THE first person Glen had confided in about his childhood survival story practically since it happened, having reached the conclusion when he was still young that it was a story that ought not to be shared, based on the alienation of his peers.

But he told Jade about it early in their relationship, when she had initiated one of her chakra healing activities that involved disclosing past traumas and the burning of sage.

Glen gathered that the *disclosure* aspect of the activity was not voluntary.

So he began to tell her the story of Ramses and the woods and the snow but as he did he worried that she would realize he was stupid, or fear he might be volatile, or reject him for some unspoken reason as his classmates had.

But Jade wasn't fazed, at all. As a matter of fact, she said the nicest thing. She said that in her view, brain damage was yet another unique feature about Glen and in fact was almost like a boon if you looked at it a certain way; a blessing from the universe, a shortcut to magical thinking.

SHANNON SAID: "COME on, Glen. We're out of here. She's going to accuse us of stealing, then nitpick and insult us? Let's—"

"No," Glen said.

Both of them looked at him.

Glen knew Shannon meant well, but he would not follow her down this path. He had not stolen, he had not done anything wrong, and he did not want things to fall to pieces during dinner service, even if it would serve Orsa right. He wanted John Grisham to enjoy his meal. He said, "I don't want to leave. I just want to do my job."

The anger drained unceremoniously from Shannon's face as Orsa shot her a triumphant look.

Then Shannon frowned, leaning toward Orsa for a closer look at Orsa's notepad, where something had caught her attention. Shannon gasped.

Orsa moved to gather the notepad to her chest but not before Shannon saw it clearly enough to verify. "Oh my God," Shannon said, releasing a short scream of a laugh. "Julia?" She stared at Orsa.

Turning to Glen, Shannon said, "The only names that haven't been crossed out are yours, mine, Willis, and *Julia*." She hissed the name with bewitched delight.

Orsa exhaled through her nose with annoyance.

Shannon said again, "Julia?!"

Orsa clicked her pen a few times. "Look. I don't want to fight with you anymore. Either of you. This interrogation is over." She put the notepad back on the desk and made a real show of crossing out their names. "Glen," she said, "I don't think you've got it in you; I never did. And Shannon, I don't think it's the kind of statement you'd make, even if you really felt you had a statement to make."

Shannon said, "True." She nodded at the list with her jutted-out chin. "So what are we going to do about it, now that you have it narrowed down to two?"

Orsa said, "Keep our eyes and ears peeled."

Shannon said, "Roger that."

Orsa's phone vibrated and she peered down at it. "Oh, good, that'll be Larry with my steaks." She looked back and forth between Glen and Shannon. "So are we all good then? Because . . . I just need to make sure we're good. I don't want you walking out. Not tonight. Or writing about me on Facebook. *Capisce*?"

Glen said, "Okay."

Shannon said, "We're so good."

Orsa said, "I'm glad we hashed things out. A heart-to-heart. I know sometimes it's hard for you guys to see me as any more than your boss, but I see you as much more than my employees."

Shannon said, "If you say so."

Shannon and Glen walked out of Orsa's office together.

Back in the kitchen, Shannon said, "I really would've thought you'd pick me over her, Glennie." She *tsk*ed her tongue. "But I should've known you wouldn't ever follow me out of this place. I should've known."

While the words themselves were not particularly unkind, Glen sensed something a little bit ugly in the message. He wasn't sure, though. Shannon was his friend. He was so bad at differentiating between words and meanings when they were not the same.

He said, "It's not about you versus her."

"I know."

"I can't leave," Glen said. "I can't. I can't . . ." He struggled to make Shannon understand. "I'm not like you."

"I know," she said again. She patted his elbow fondly before they parted ways to return to their separate stations.

Back at his station, Glen returned to his chimichurri. It was not his personal favorite sauce option; that was the red wine jus. He could appreciate that the chimichurri was aromatic and fresh and vibrant in color, but there were so many things that could go wrong. The flavor had to be perfect or it was terrible, and even if you followed the recipe to a tee, variables such as overripe herbs or old garlic or extra hot chilis could throw off the balance. And the parsley rinse had to be thorough; the tiniest bit of grit would ruin a bite, possibly even the meal. The other issue with the chimichurri was presentation—it required a good shake and stir before application, otherwise the yellowy oil would separate from the solids.

Glen rinsed several times then roughly chopped the parsley and tossed it into the food processor. To this he added garlic, red wine vinegar, olive oil, jalapeños, oregano, salt and pepper.

Chef Oz wasn't in the kitchen so Glen tasted it himself, added another clove of garlic, called it perfect and transferred it to a plastic quart canister. He dated it with masking tape and put it in the fridge then washed the implements he'd used.

Back at his station Glen wiped at a bright green smear on his apron and took off his hat to smooth his hairnet underneath it. Others in the kitchen played fast and loose with food safety rules, such as the covering of hair, unless they knew they were due for an inspection. Chef Oz was the most flagrant offender, not that he had that much hair to cover. Glen didn't have all that much hair either but he didn't understand why anyone would take the risk.

He had used his nakiri knife on the parsley and lifted it now to eye level to see if it needed to be sharpened. The even gleam of it under the fluorescent light gave him a jolt of satisfaction.

Glen knew what people said about him—*lifer*—that word whispered like it was worse than a curse or an overt insult. But, he thought, admiring the monogramming on his knife: *My life is my own!*

He had not done anything wrong, and he would not be bullied out of this restaurant, either by Orsa or by Shannon. He would not budge, and he would not surrender—not one inch, to anyone. As a matter of fact, he thought, if he never heard the word *surrender*, or *sacred*, or *soul*, again in his life, that would be just fine. Because he knew now that he was the opposite of magical; he was a man entirely of this world. And his life was his own.

THE BUSSER

THE PHARMACEUTICAL RESERVATION WAS FOR five thirty, meaning the rep would arrive at five or shortly after, so Ant scarfed the staff meal—noodles with ground beef and alfredo sauce made from powder—and went out to the patio to help Byron who would serve the table, to make sure everything was in order. Ant was a hustler by nature, a small, double-jointed kid who drank two Monsters before every shift.

"Hey, Ant," Byron said without looking at him. "Did you hear?"

"Grisham Day, right?" Bussers were not required to attend the shift meeting that always took place just before staff meal, when specials and eighty-sixes and noteworthy reservations were discussed. Bussers didn't need to know any of this. They didn't need to know anything except how to do what the servers told them to do.

"Well, yes," Byron said, "Grisham Day. But no. More importantly, did you hear about dish?"

Ant shook his head.

"The dishwasher's down," Byron said. "Out of order. Happened right before staff meeting—Glen ran some of his implements and the thing acted like it was going to back up, then it shut off altogether and won't turn on. Nobody's got time to get in there with the toolbox. Or the know-how."

"So what does that mean for us?"

"Darius handles all the glassware in the bar and as much other stuff as he's able to run, to help us out. Everything that would go through the kitchen, Willis does by hand."

"Good God," Ant said.

"He's running late, too, Willis; should be here already. But that's nothing new. Hey, can you swap out the spoon on seat nine?"

"Sure thing."

Byron said, "And I'd advise you stay out of Orsa's way unless you want an earful about the wrinkles in your shirt. Between Grisham, the dishwasher, and the steaks, she's a hair away from slitting somebody's throat over just about anything."

Ant said, "What steaks?"

"Shit," Byron said, then took a few paces so they were closer and he could whisper. "Somebody stole a bunch of steaks on Saturday," he explained. "Don't worry, you're not on the short list of suspects, pal. I wasn't supposed to say anything. Mouth shut?"

Ant nodded. "Steaks, though? Weird."

"This place is full of weirdos."

Ant did a quick walk-around of the whole long table to make sure there were no more errors in the settings that would require a replacement, before heading back to the kitchen for a soup spoon to replace the dessert spoon. On his way he straightened silver, re-formed a drooping clamshell, flicked a tiny brown spider off the linen.

Nearby Byron was kneeling to fix the wobble in one of the six two-tops that were pushed together to create the table, when his wine key fell from his pocket. Ant was closer and retrieved it. He admired its heft and wooden detailing. "This thing's nice, man," he observed, returning it to Byron.

"Does the job."

"Where'd you get it?"

Byron pushed on the corner of the wobbly table to see if he'd corrected the balance. "Beats me," he said, putting the wine key back in his pocket.

In the kitchen, Willis had just arrived and was approaching the dish pit from the opposite direction as Ant. He straightened and tied his apron, rubbed his red eyes.

When Chef Oz made his way toward the dish pit Ant kept his distance but made sure he had a good vantage point while sifting through polished silver.

Chef Oz said to Willis, "Yo, the unit's down." He banged the stainless steel with his knuckles. "As of just a few minutes ago. Tried to plunge just in case it's a loose blockage, but nothing came out and it won't turn on now. We don't know if it's plumbing or the unit, nobody's got time to get in there, and we can't risk making a bigger problem by forcing it or tinkering around. So it's off-limits until it's been cleared. Repair guy's on the way but he's out on another call and might be a while."

Willis blinked slowly, like a cow. "So, this means . . . ?"

"What I just said, numb nuts," Oz said.

"And what does this mean for me?"

"Darius will handle glassware in the bar, servers will all go to him for that, and he can probably keep up with some silver and other small stuff, too. But once bar traffic picks up, he's not going to be much help. We're on our own for everything he can't handle."

"Meaning . . ."

"Meaning," Oz said, pointing to an unopened packet of scrubby sponges on the far side of the sink, "you'll be handwashing. And it's Grisham Day, and we've got a pharma dinner twenty-top, so it's gonna be a busy one. Hut-hut."

Willis looked at the sponges then back at Oz. "You're shitting me," he said.

"I wish I was," Oz said. He grabbed a kitchen rag and snapped it at Willis's legs. "Get to it, Cinderella."

Chef Oz turned back toward his station.

Ant watched as Willis eyed the sponges one more time.

Then he watched as Willis untied his apron, lifted the neck strap over his head, and deposited it unceremoniously into the dirty linen basket. He called toward the line, "Yo, Chef, fuck this, I'm out of here."

Chef Oz spun away from the stove to stare at Willis. "Funny stuff. Get that apron back on."

Willis was already walking back to the basement stairway.

Glen was staring. Shannon was staring.

Willis blew a kiss to the whole kitchen. "Sayonara, sweeties," he called.

A dark silence descended on the room.

Ant slipped out of the kitchen to avoid being present for Chef Oz's full wrath.

On the patio he breathlessly delivered the news to Byron who promptly stormed toward the kitchen, presumably to confirm.

Byron returned shortly after, shaking his head.

Ant said, "What's the plan?"

"We've managed without a dishwasher once or twice before," Byron said. "Everybody pitches in when they have a free moment. Shannon will probably do the bulk of it with Glen covering for her when he can. It won't be pretty. And Chef Oz's probably going to try and co-opt you for dish duty every time you come through the kitchen for something, but just tell him to back off; you're helping me deal with a twenty-top out here."

"What time is Grisham coming?"

"Not til seven, fortunately. So, we should have entrees on the pharma table, maybe even cleared, before Grisham's even putting his order in. That should help with the flow. Kenzie's got a handful of rezzies between now and seven, but nothing big. So, you're really gonna be my right hand til Grisham's here."

Ant said, "Sure, boss."

When servers rationalized to Ant why they should be his top priority for any given shift, he always responded agreeably. It wasn't worth pointing out what was going on elsewhere in the restaurant that might also require his attention. If there was one thing he'd learned in his six months working at a restaurant, it was that it was never, ever worth arguing with anyone at a restaurant.

Ant said, "I'm surprised you're not on the Grisham table. Being a writer and all, I'd've thought you'd want it."

"Orsa wanted Rhea on it," Byron said. He gestured toward the table before them. "This one's going to be twice as much money and half the fuss. There's no way I want the Grisham table anyway. Guy's a hack."

Ant said, "My mom's obsessed with him. She's read every single one of his books, seen all the movies, has all her opinions about them. I'm pretty sure she's actually sent him fan mail. When I told her he was coming to the restaurant back when the reservation was made, she went straight to the calendar. I told her, *No way*; that even the staff isn't allowed to look at him except for the person taking his order. She would've shown up in her Sunday best with thirty books for him to sign if I hadn't put my foot down."

Byron mimicked a gag.

Ant didn't mind working for Byron or Rhea or any of the servers, really. They were all nice enough, especially compared to some of the abuse his buddies who worked at Red Lobster endured, but if Ant had his way, they'd all be Kenzies. She looked like a real-life Barbie, smelled like cotton candy, and her service standards were exceptionally low. She wouldn't notice a dessert spoon set out instead of a soup spoon, for instance, and if she did notice she wouldn't care. Kenzie's tip percentage did not seem to suffer from her inattentiveness. Lately, Kenzie often seemed to end up serving the late tables the servers typically tried to fob off, so she and Ant had finished up a number of recent shifts working side by side, just the two of them in an otherwise empty dining room. Ant was still in high school, a pip-squeak who didn't—wouldn't ever—stand a chance with a girl like Kenzie, but that didn't preclude his fantasies in these scenarios.

In any case, Ant existed comfortably in his role here. He worked hard enough to earn his tip-out and hopefully a positive reference for future employment, but stayed out of the fray. He didn't care to ingratiate himself socially. He was a kid. His friends were kids. He lived with his parents and younger siblings, one of whom was still in diapers. Homework and college applications and *Skyrim* were his priorities. Occasionally, exciting things happened at the restaurant that he could report to his friends, such as John Grisham making a reservation or Kenzie's bra becoming unhooked, but outside of the actual hours he spent there, the job was far from his mind.

THE PHARMACEUTICAL REP showed up at five after five, right as a deuce and a four-top were going down in Kenzie's section, and Julia put a walk-in deuce in Rhea's section since in theory she would have them in and out before the Grisham table arrived. Two doctors arrived early and eager for a drink on the patio, even though the rep had not even begun to set up her projection system.

For the next hour and a half, Ant ran on caffeine and adrenaline, swirling through space and time, dining room, kitchen and bar.

Watering, clearing, silvering, another Pepsi—*Is Coke okay? I'm sorry about that*, more ice, less ice, *Let me get your server, he'll be able to answer that for you*, and *Just down that hallway and on the left*, and *May I clear your plate?* A clean spoon, a fresh napkin, *Oopsies, let me help you with your seat*, and *It's really a matter of personal preference, ma'am. I just couldn't say. No, I just really couldn't make that decision for you. Would you like me to get your server?* More coffee, more cream, more coffee. *As far as I know, that's always been the portion size, but I've only been here for about six months.*

At the pharma table: matter-of-fact talk of fistulas. Children at table Nine, so get the bread out extra fast, or not, oh no, no bread, the girl has celiac, get that bread off that table, immediately, replace with berries. Just, fresh and raw. Ask Shannon. Shannon doesn't have extras? Rinse and stem a bowl yourself if you need them so bad, you know where to find them in the walk-in. The mom wants to know if there'll be an upcharge for berries instead of bread because if so, don't even worry about it because the girl won't eat more than a few. But if they are complimentary and you do intend to bring them out please wash your hands if you've been handling bread because even just a crumb can set her off. *Happy anniversary to you both. No, unfortunately, typically we don't do anything, but yes, I'll make sure your server is aware.* ENTREES UP ON ELEVEN, DESSERTS ON FOUR, I NEED A RUNNER YESTERDAY, THIS SHIT IS GROWING MOLD. Here's my credit card, add 18 percent, make sure the bill never shows up at the table, I tried to give it to the server but couldn't catch her eye. Ah, for Christ's sakes, Ant, why'd you take the card? You know I hate this shit, doesn't matter if I run the card, return it, don't even print the bill, they'll still make me bear witness to the dick-swinging for a full fifteen minutes. Well, where is the card then? An AMEX? We don't even take that! Ah, for Christ's sakes, Ant. *More bread? Certainly... I'm afraid we just have this one type of butter, I'm so sorry. But there is the salt, just here, if you'd care to add a pinch yourself...*

If it was chaotic in the dining room, it was absolute mayhem in the kitchen. Shannon and Glen were hopping off the line to deal with dishes when they had a free moment, as well as front-of-housers as they were able. Rhea hand-washed and dried bread plates for the pharma dinner, Darius handled all of the glassware he went through himself at the bar, Glen hand-washed what he and Oz and Shannon needed. Still, rack after rack of dishes piled up. A six-top walk-in arrived, and Rhea was the only server in a position to handle them so she greeted them, even though it meant the group would overlap with the Grisham table which was supposed to be her only working table at the time of their arrival. Shannon burned another brûlée and dropped a quart of caramel sauce. Glen covered her station while she cleaned up, but she did a bad job and the floor turned tacky. Oz and Byron had a full-on shouting match about extra peppercorn sauce on the side. One of the heat lamps flickered, threatening to die. The hinge on the swinging door between kitchen and dining room had loosened again and it went off like a gunshot every time anyone slammed through it.

Orsa was on the floor and attempting to help, or something like that, but although she popped in to oversee a dinner shift often enough to understand the overall operation, she was never actually part of it; she didn't have a clue what to do with herself and was in everyone's way. After burning her hand on an entree plate, very nearly dropping an entire rack of dripping coffee cups, and misreading a ticket aloud to Oz, which messed up not only one entree but timing for the entire table, she was at her breaking point. Her glasses were foggy. Ant had never seen her hair get messed up before.

At six thirty, just before entrees were about to get plated for the pharma table, Orsa issued a mandate she'd never before been known to give: she told Julia not to seat any more walk-ins, even though there were a few vacant tables, so that they could get things under control before Grisham's arrival.

It was the right move, Ant thought. The flow was off. Byron and Chef Oz, like a couple of toddlers, weren't speaking to each other, which left Ant to deliver essential messages about the large party. Everyone was sweating and cussing and guzzling iced coffees. They desperately needed a few minutes to get things under control before Grisham's arrival.

Once the pharma entrees had gone out though, everything settled down. Ant helped Byron make the rounds to water the table and confirm that entrees were to everyone's liking.

By six forty-five, the doctors enjoying their entrees, fresh drinks all around, an almost eerie calm had settled over the place.

Ant sniffed his armpits, drank some Sprite, then made his way through the restaurant to see if anyone was still behind and in need of a hand. In the kitchen, he polished some silver and grabbed linens for resets.

In the server station, Kenzie and Rhea were looking at a piece of paper that Kenzie's deuce at Fourteen had just handed her.

Rhea stared at the paper. "You've got to be kidding me,"

she cackled. "Oh my God. Look, there's not even a bar code or anything, just this random number. Oh my God. The different fonts... I can't believe they handed this to you. What was their tab?"

Kenzie glanced at their receipt in her server book. "Ninety-two."

"What are they like?"

"Nothings. Literal no ones."

Rhea folded the paper up and returned it to Kenzie. "Take it back to the table, tell them you showed it to the manager, and confirmed it's invalid. If they act like they're not prepared to pay or ask to talk to management directly, I'll swing by."

Ant asked, "What's with Fourteen?"

Kenzie said, "They're either frauds or morons."

Rhea said to her, "I'm guessing you're getting stiffed on a tip either way."

Kenzie growled.

"Sorry, babe," Rhea said. "Find me if you need me to talk to them."

Kenzie turned to Ant. "Can you make two double espressos and drop them at Eleven while I deal with Fourteen?"

"Sure thing."

The next time Ant made his way through Kenzie's section of the dining room with the espressos for Eleven, he attempted to sneak a glance at the frauds or morons—the nothings—at Fourteen, whom he had tended to earlier in their meal but they had indeed failed to leave an impression—he couldn't recall a single thing about them. By the time he went looking, they were already gone.

When he passed the host stand, he observed that Julia wore an expression of consternation as she hung up the phone and stared at the screen before her.

He sidled up next to her. "Do you think I should go ahead and water the Grisham table or wait a few more minutes?"

"Don't bother. The lady who made the reservation just called to cancel."

Ant's eyes widened. "Really? Orsa's gonna lose it!"

"She's been so weird to me today, too. Extra on my ass."

Ant had a glancing thought about the steak theft. Surely, Julia was not a suspect. He was tempted to gossip about it with her but thought on the off chance that she was one of the suspects who hadn't yet been informed, he'd better leave it be. He said, "Did the lady say why? That'll probably soften the blow. Grisham got sick? Delayed at the event?"

"She said they 'changed their minds.'" Julia did quotation marks with her fingers. "She apologized for the late notice."

"Changed their minds?" Ant made a face. "Yikes."

Julia agreed. "I need to find Orsa. Unless you want to deliver the news. I'll pay you twenty bucks."

"Really?"

"Five," Julia said.

"Ten."

"Deal."

Ant laughed. "Don't worry about the money. I'll tell her. What do I care? She doesn't even know who I am. I'll go tell her right now, I'll say you got stuck on another call."

"Seriously?" Julia looked at him with genuine appreciation. "You're my favorite, Ant. I've always said so."

Before he headed off toward Orsa's office, the jingle of bells at the doorway alerted Ant to someone's entry.

It was not Grisham or a walk-in but Larry, Orsa's husband. He wore a fuzzy yellow sweater and resembled a baby duck. He carried a leather briefcase over his shoulder.

Upon entering the restaurant, Larry smoothed his white hair, looking back and forth between Ant and Julia. He said, "Is Grisham here?"

"Hi, Larry," Julia said. "No, he's not."

Ant offered, "Orsa's in her office, though, I'm headed there now."

Larry said, "I'll have a drink first."

Ant watched the baby duck waddle down the hall in the opposite direction for a scotch.

Julia and Ant exchanged a look. "Godspeed," she said.

Before heading to Orsa's office, Ant paused for a breath. He stared out the front door, where the sky had darkened to a deep but still vibrant blue.

He entertained himself briefly with the theory that Larry had been the steak thief. Jealous of Orsa's obsession with John Grisham and the lengths taken to ensure Grisham's perfect meal, Larry had decided to throw a wrench into her day.

Ant's dad found his mom's obsession with Grisham hilarious. Back when Ant demanded his mother not show up tonight for a glimpse, his dad had tried to goad her into doing it anyway.

Ant stretched, cracked his knuckles, looked at the clock and yawned. Now that one big push was over, he had no desire to endure a second one, even if another wave of guests would mean a bigger tip-out. He was now ready for things to slowly wind down. He'd be glad if helping to clear the pharma dinner, silver them for dessert, then clean up and do resets after they were gone were the only real remaining tasks for the night. Operating without a dishwasher had proven a greater strain than Ant might have guessed, given how much loafing about Willis seemed to do most nights.

In any case, Ant's mind had already moved past the shift and toward more pressing concerns. He had physics homework and a text thread to catch up on—one of his buddies had scored some weed. He was hungry for whatever leftovers his mom would have waiting at home on a plate in the fridge. He needed to work on one of his college application essays. The focus of the essay was to describe an event that had sparked deep personal growth in his life.

Ant had not put a lot of thought into the topic, but thus far nothing had sprung to mind. It struck him as a ridiculous conceit. *Deep personal growth in his life?* For all intents and purposes, Ant thought, his actual life had not yet even begun. Most of the time Ant felt like he was still dangling a foot over the side of the river that would eventually sweep him up and carry him to more, and greater, and final destinations. This feeling was perhaps, Ant realized now, why he didn't care much to engage with the rest of the staff at Aunt O's—because he had the sense that the opposite was true for most of them, and this was too depressing to even contemplate. With a few exceptions—such as Kenzie—it seemed to Ant that for his coworkers, the river had already taken them for their ride and spat them out on the far side.

THE NEXT TIME Ant would think of this moment would be thirty-some years later when he was living in a large city and working as an orthopedic surgeon, attending a dinner with various colleagues at a nice restaurant where an attractive pharmaceutical rep was presenting on a new type of acrylic bone cement that had been developed for hip replacements. Anthony Webster, MD, would not be at the event because he had any real intention of utilizing this technology in its very early stages of FDA approval, but because his wife, who he dearly loved, was divorcing him, his teenage children were no longer willing to sit at the dinner table with him, and he'd rather attend one of these silly events for the free steak and nice Cab and cute presenter than dine alone in his home yet again. As Dr. Webster would watch a busboy make his way around the table of doctors with water, the recollection of sweating in a cheap starched shirt while pouring water from an unwieldy stainless-steel pitcher would reach him viscerally, along with the memory of the conversation he'd had with himself on Grisham Day, about life, its befores and afters. He would realize with disbelief that here he was, on the other side of the river, spat out on the far side of life, with no memory of ever having crossed it. His heart would sink. He would wonder, *My God, my God, what was I doing instead of noticing?*

THE DINERS

TABLE FOURTEEN SEAT #1 LET HIS WIFE DO the talking at the host stand. It wasn't like she had any more experience with this kind of thing—fine dining—than he did, but she was more outgoing of the two and she was the one that had called for the reservation, though she put it under his name.

They were seated at a table located next to a window that faced directly into a ratty winterberry shrub and beyond that, out across the parking lot.

Seat #2 ran her hand over the white tablecloth and gazed through the dining room then at the square brass votive in the center of the table. She had put her short hair in curlers for the first time in many years, and the small gray coils glowed around her face.

Seat #1 was thirsty but afraid to lift his water glass,

which was goblet shaped and so full that the slightest tremor would result in a spill.

Seat #2 said, "Gail told me that the one time they came, she ordered a drink that had cayenne pepper floating in it."

Seat #1 said, "You want something like that?"

Seat #2 shook her head. "I thought I'd do a glass of white. I was just saying."

"I wasn't saying you shouldn't." Seat #1 pulled his reading glasses from his breast pocket and put them on then took them off. "I'm just gonna do the soup of the day as long as it's nothing weird, and a steak, like I saw on the website."

Seat #2 said, "You don't even want to think about something else, or hear the specials?"

Seat #1 said, "I know what I like. But you do whatever you want, dear. I'm not trying to be a grump." He shifted in his seat and stared at the artwork hanging nearest to their table: an abstract work of a horselike form emerging from red and gold splatter. "It's hard for me to relax, a place like this. Did you see the vehicles parked in the lot?"

"Nope," Seat #2 said cheerfully. She hummed and tipped her head back and forth as she examined the menu. She had read it in advance on the website, too, so Seat #1 didn't know what she was looking for.

Their server introduced herself as Kenzie. Blonde with perfect teeth and dimples, she was uncannily pretty. Seat #1 thought girls who looked like this belonged only to TV.

Kenzie took their drink order and asked if they had any questions about the menu.

Seat #2 said, "Kenzie, that's a beautiful name. It suits you."

Seat #1 said, "What's the soup?"

Seat #2 said, "And I'd love to hear all your specials."

Kenzie opened her little black bifold book and read: "Soup of the day is a butternut squash. The only special is an appetizer, a stuffed portobello mushroom with sausage, peppers, and Gruyère."

Seat #1 knew that Seat #2 wouldn't touch a mushroom but he watched as she licked her lips and said, "Sounds yummy."

When Kenzie brought their beer and wine, they made their order: two soups and two steaks, both medium-well.

Once Kenzie had left the table, Seat #1 took a few big swallows of beer and felt better. He forgot how numb his toes had gone in the narrow dress shoes Seat #2 had encouraged him to wear.

He reached across the table for his wife's fingers and squeezed them.

She said, "Are you enjoying yourself?"

"I'm trying."

"Good," she said. "That's the point. Remember?" She let go of his hands and took a sip of wine. "Remember?"

"I remember."

She lifted her napkin to her lips and dabbed them then returned the napkin to her lap. "I really think this time it's gonna stick. I have such a good feeling about it."

"Okay," said Seat #1.

"We went to a place sort of like this that one time with my brother, in New Jersey, remember?"

"I remember."

"I think we both had chicken, didn't we? And lots of bread. But mostly what I remember is how good the piano player was. That Italian man. What about you?"

Seat #1 said, "Mostly I remember how good you thought the Italian piano player was."

Seat #2 laughed. "Silly."

Seat #1 burned his tongue on the soup. Once it cooled down, he could appreciate the flavor, but it didn't strike him as anything special, and the color was like throw-up.

Seat #2 claimed it was the best soup she'd ever had.

Seat #1 said, "I like your chili better."

"You're a crazy man."

He insisted, "You could make this."

"Maybe. But I don't guess I'm allowed to ask for a recipe in a place like this."

Seat #1 said, "I bet if we look on the computer, we can find some recipes that'll taste like it, or close. You can find anything you want on there."

They watched as a couple was seated nearby, the woman very round with pregnancy. The man helped with her chair and kissed the crown of her head.

When Kenzie returned for their soup bowls, Seat #2 said to her, "Did you get to taste it before your shift? It's incredible." She added conspiratorially, "You should sneak a bite if you haven't already."

Kenzie said, "I don't really like soup, like, in general."

Seat #1 and Seat #2 both ordered a second drink. After delivering them, Kenzie disappeared for a long spell while they awaited their steaks.

They talked about the new neighbor who shaved one whole side of her head, clean down to the skin, and wore the other half in a blue braid. Seat #2 said, "She really does do such a nice job with her nasturtiums, though. I'd trust her with our watering if we ever leave town long enough to need it." She sipped her wine. "She reminds me of that Sarah girl Jimmy brought around for a while. Do you remember her?"

"Haven't thought about that one in ages," Seat #1 said.

"I wonder if he'll start dating again soon, now that—"

"Who knows."

They talked about the incumbent mayor's new campaign ad which featured some footage of his terrier running through the park, with the mayor's wife doing voice-over. They liked the guy but agreed the ad was off-putting. They talked about how their fortieth anniversary was next summer already somehow and agreed they ought to figure out soon how to celebrate. Seat #1 was glad Seat #2 didn't suggest a repeat meal at this place, though that didn't mean it wouldn't come up at some point down the road.

They talked about the great horned owl they heard high up in the ash tree to the west of their house every single night around eight o'clock. Seat #2 had read recently that a great horned owl could live to be fifty years old. They talked about the current challenges of the food pantry operation, which Seat #2 oversaw at church.

Still their food had not arrived.

Seat #2 said hopefully, "We did order medium-well."

"True."

"And I bet they're really thick cuts. Sixteen ounces. Golly." She leaned back and rubbed her belly.

They waited and waited.

Kenzie and several other waitstaff rushed through the dining room looking harried although only half of the available tables in this section of the dining room were seated. Seat #1 noticed some other guests looking around, too, waiting and wondering.

When the busboy stopped by with water, Seat #2 said pleasantly, "Busy night?"

The busboy was sweating. "Twenty-top on the patio," he said. "Their entrees just came up. I'm sure yours will be next."

Seat #2 assured him that she wasn't worried. "We're enjoying ourselves so much." She added, "It's our first time."

The busboy said, "Celebrating something?"

Seat #2 said, "Well, yes!" at the exact same moment that Seat #1 said, "Not really."

They looked at one another and laughed.

The busboy removed their empty glasses and said, "Would you like another round? I can let Kenzie know if I catch her before you do."

Seat #2 said, "Should we?"

"If you like."

"I do."

"I'll have one, too, then."

Seat #1 looked around once again and observed that they were the oldest people in the place by quite a ways. They were also dressed the most formally; Seat #2 in her blue dress and blazer and that huge necklace, Seat #1 in a tie. Plenty of other guests wore jeans, and some even T-shirts.

The busboy returned shortly with their entree plates, one in each hand, a white napkin draped over his left forearm.

The steaks were fatty and incomprehensibly large. "My word," said Seat #2, staring at the thing.

Kenzie showed up momentarily with their fresh drinks.

"I'm sorry about the wait," she said. "A big table had their entrees come out right before yours. And there was an injury in the kitchen."

"Oh dear," Seat #2 said. "Is everyone alright?"

Kenzie said, "Who knows. Anything else I can get you right now?"

Seat #1 and #2 clinked their glasses together after Kenzie left the table.

Seat #2 said, "If we're toasting to anything, it ought to be to Jimmy, right? For all of this." She swept her hand out over the table of food.

Seat #1 grunted and sipped his beer. He knew he should be grateful. He knew he should be enjoying himself. He knew he should have hope. For Seat #2's sake, he tried.

They both picked around and ate a few ounces, but the sheer volume of meat on the plate was too much to really appreciate. Seat #2 poked with her knife. "The soup was just so rich. The steak is absolutely perfect, but I'm so full." Seat #1 thought his wife was so determined to have a perfect time she wouldn't say a bad word about this meal if they brought out a bowl of hair.

"Me too," said Seat #1.

When Kenzie returned to check in a while later, Seat #1 asked for to-go bags. He planned to give his meat to the dog.

Seat #2 said, "It was incredible, we're just stuffed to the gills. I can't wait to finish this later at home."

"No dessert menus, then?" Kenzie asked.

Seat #2 said, "Maybe just to look."

After Kenzie dropped dessert menus, Seat #2 said to Seat #1, "I think we ought to treat ourselves. Besides, I think we're only at eighty-five or so."

Seat #1 hadn't been doing math but trusted hers.

Seat #2 said, "Would you split a crème brûlée with me?"

"Whatever you want, honey," he said. He had zero interest in dessert but was pleased that his wife was keen to spend the full gift card balance on this visit, meaning there would be no reason to return.

"Goodie," she said.

Seat #2 gobbled up the brûlée. She set her spoon down and said, "Now I'm truly about to burst."

Seat #1 caught Kenzie's eye. He made a "check" motion with his hand.

Before Kenzie had returned with it, Seat #2 pulled her purse from the shoulder of her chair and withdrew her pocketbook.

The gift certificate was neatly folded; Seat #2 pressed it on the top of the table.

Kenzie approached with a black bifold which she rested on their table half opened and said, "When you're ready."

Seat #2 handed her the paper and announced, "We've got this."

Kenzie gazed at the paper and gave it a funny look. "Um . . ." she said. "They don't look like this."

Seat #2 said, "Oh, what now?"

Kenzie said, "Our gift cards are always a physical card. That we can, like, actually run through our machine."

Seat #2 said, "Oh, but . . . Well, we did think this looked

a little strange when we received it, but everything's digital nowadays . . . We just thought . . ."

Kenzie said neutrally, "I'll go ask my manager to make sure. But to me, I've never seen . . . This isn't . . . Well, anyhow, I will show it to my manager just to make sure."

She reached for the paper.

A ferocious shame and familiar rage was rising inside of Seat #1.

It was a sheet of normal computer paper with the restaurant's logo in black and white and the words: "Gift Card for the value of $100" followed by a very long number. No expiration date, no bar code. Seat #1 had commented back upon receiving it, once it was just the two of them of course, that it looked kind of strange and unprofessional. Seat #2 had pointed out, "But everything is done electronic like this nowadays. It's got their actual logo on it, see? I'm sure this big, long number is the important part." Seat #1 said, "I guess you're right."

Confusion crumpling her face, Seat #2 was somehow still talking to Kenzie: "I just don't understand . . . See, we received it as a gift from . . ." her voice trailed off. She said, "And he's had his problems, but we thought . . ." But Kenzie had already spun away from the table with the paper in hand.

Seat #1 leaned over to one side to pull out his wallet and said flatly, "I guess we learned our lesson. Again." He counted six twenties and put them on the table. "Here. Let's just leave this cash and go. It's enough to cover the meal and the tip. There's no way she's coming back with good news, and I'd rather not have to talk about it again. Or sit and wait while she runs a credit card."

Seat #2 stared at him. "You never carry that much cash," she said.

Seat #1 exhaled. "I just figured, better to be prepared for anything."

"You just figured, did you?" Seat #2 drummed her fingertips on the top of her to-go box and gazed out the window for a moment, looking like she would cry. Sometimes she still needed to cry over things like this, sometimes she didn't.

Seat #1 said, "I'm sorry. I love you." He had no idea what else to say. He was so full of love and pain that he could have thrown his old fist through the window.

Seat #2 did not cry. Instead, she said, "Oh, well. Oh, well then." She pulled the napkin from her lap onto the table and folded it neatly. She sighed. "Let's go home," she said. She looked at her watch. "The owl will be coming out soon."

Seat #1 said, "Don't want to miss that."

He followed his wife out of the dining room. He noticed that her hose had a little run at the left ankle.

To Seat #1's relief, they did not pass either Kenzie or a manager on the way, but in the lobby the hostess called to them, "How was everything tonight, folks?"

Seat #2 lifted her head to say, "We loved it. Everything was perfect."

THE INVESTOR

LARRY WASN'T A FANATIC BUT HE WAS A FAN. Back when the reservation was made Orsa had forbade Larry from making an appearance during the shift—she said he'd make it weird—and he had intended to comply. But now that things had gone sideways with the steaks and all, he figured he'd bought himself some goodwill by running around town all afternoon, picking up replacement rib eyes. So after dropping them off with her, he went home, showered and shaved, with plans to enjoy an evening scotch back at the restaurant, as he often did. While there, maybe he'd have a stroll through the place to say hello to the staff, and look, if it happened that Grisham and Larry crossed paths in the bar or the dining room or the men's room or parking lot, Larry would happen to have a Sharpie and his hardcover copy of *The Pelican Brief* at the ready. Maybe they'd talk law school a little bit, or the movie adaptation of *A Time to Kill*. Larry wondered if Grisham had gotten to spend time on set and chat with Sandra Bullock. Larry's first wife, Diane, had looked a bit like 1990s Sandra Bullock when they met in the 1970s. But nowadays Diane's hair was as white as snow and cut very short to her head. Larry knew this from Facebook, where they were Friends, unlike in real life, where they'd had no contact for decades. Along with her current hairstyle Larry also knew from Facebook that Diane was a liberal, a widow, a painter of watercolors. Now and then, she posted a picture of her artwork. The paintings were so bad that Larry's heart just about broke every time he looked at them. He always pressed "Like" then stared at the computer for a while to see if anything else was going to happen.

Anyway, that was all in the past. No point dwelling on Diane's paintings or her new or old hair.

As for today and the matter at hand, well, Orsa would give Larry the dickens for showing up. But later, next week sometime, she'd be over it and might even be grateful to have the autographed book as a memento. Besides—Larry didn't like to pull this card very often—but it *was* technically his restaurant. So while he was usually fine to let Orsa do things her way and boss him around like one of her employees, on occasion he exerted his authority behind the scenes. Today was such an occasion. If John Grisham was going to dine in his restaurant, Larry would be damned if he wasn't going to at least set eyes on the guy.

When Larry entered the restaurant, though, he was informed by Julia the host that Grisham wasn't there yet.

Julia wore a silky collared shirt and her dark hair was

pulled into a ponytail. Larry liked Julia. Not quite as much as he liked Kenzie, the blonde server, but Julia always greeted him with a smile. Those two were about the only names he could ever remember.

Today, though, Julia did not have a smile for Larry. Larry figured they were all probably under the gun with Grisham stress.

Larry walked to the bar, ordered his usual from Darius, crossed back through the foyer and made his way to Orsa's office.

When he entered, Larry was taken aback by the grim expression his wife wore, before she had even fully registered his presence. When she did, she muttered, "Close that door behind you, SpongeBob."

Larry pulled the door shut behind him and took a seat across from her. "Hi, honey," he said, amiably.

"What the hell are you wearing?" she said. "Really trying to fly under the radar here, aren't you, Mister Don't-Worry-I-Wouldn't-Even-Dream-Of-Showing-Up?"

Larry looked down at the backs of his hands and fluffed the hair on his knuckles. "I know you didn't want me to come, but I'm a fan. It's a big deal, a once in a lifetime chance. And I wish you wouldn't ever make me remind you of this, but the place *is* technically—"

"He's not coming," Orsa cut in.

"Oh," Larry said. "Grisham, really? Canceled?"

"Perhaps," Orsa said, and Larry could see that she was truly crestfallen. "Or never was." She rubbed her eyes.

"What's that mean?"

"I'm glad you're here, actually," she said. "I need somebody to talk to. I don't know what to think. My head's spinning. The day I've had. It's got me looking sideways at everybody."

"Sure," Larry said sympathetically. "The steaks and all. But what's that got to do with Grisham?"

"Julia took the Grisham reservation," Orsa said. "Over a month ago. Allegedly. She's the one that talked to the department head's assistant, who organized Grisham's visit. And Julia's the one that called the assistant last week to confirm the reservation. Allegedly."

"Why do you keep saying that?"

"Because I've got reason to believe that she's behind the steaks, which, it seems clear now, was all just to mess with me. And now, with this reser—"

"Julia?" Larry made a face. "She's the last person—well, just about, or the second-last person—"

"I know," Orsa interrupted. "I was saying the same thing earlier today. But after reviewing the bank footage and talking to the other people who were here Saturday and had the means to get them out of the building, I've ruled out pretty much everyone else."

"What about your dishwasher, though?" Larry said. "Did you talk to him? I'd always look at the dishwasher first."

"Oh, God, I forgot, you don't even know that. The dishwasher unit crapped out after you left. It's been such a day, I can hardly keep it all straight myself. Happened right before shift meeting. It made some wretched sound apparently, seized up, and won't even turn on now."

"You're kidding."

"We've been without it for a couple hours before and made do; it wouldn't have been the end of the world today, but then when Willis showed up for his dishwashing shift at five and learned he'd be hand-washing plates and pans, he turned around and walked out."

"You're kidding!" Larry said again.

"Repairman's on the way but who knows when he'll get here."

"You've got a toolbox here, don't you?"

"Oz is the only one who I'd trust even getting near that thing," Orsa said, "and he's obviously been slammed all night."

"I could give it a look, if you—"

"You don't know a wrench from a raspberry. No offense."

Larry frowned. "I just fixed your juicer last week."

"Anyway, I don't know what to make of it. Seems like I'm getting messed with from every direction. I just can't imagine Julia taking issue with me, but in a certain light... I'm saying, what if Grisham was never coming at all and it was just a hoax to get me all wound up? All the other shenanigans, the steaks and whatnot, to make a terrible day worse. And instead of telling me herself, about the Grisham cancellation, Julia just now sent that busser whose name I can never remember, to deliver the news. Like maybe she was afraid she'd give herself away if she was looking me in the eye, and—"

Larry interrupted, "Before you go down this rabbit hole, why don't you call the number in the system for the Grisham reservation just to follow up? If it's a fake number, then you'll know the whole thing was a setup. If it's real, if somebody picks up, you'll know... Well, you'll know something different. I think you should do that before you go nailing Julia to the cross."

"You're right," Orsa said, snapping her fingers. She turned to her computer monitor, which was linked to the host stand database. Larry watched as she pulled up the floor plan and then the information associated with the canceled Grisham reservation.

Orsa dialed the call-back number into her cell phone and turned to face Larry while she waited for an answer.

"Hello," she said into the mouthpiece a moment later. "It's Orsa, from Aunt O's restaurant, where you had a reservation for tonight?" She gave Larry an affirmative nod. "Right," she said. "And I'm speaking to? Hi, Paulette. The reason for the call . . . I really appreciate your time." Orsa tapped her finger nervously on the desk calendar before her. "The reason for the call is, with the cancellation being last minute and all . . . Look, I don't want to burn any bridges. We host university groups all the time. It's just that we were just really looking forward to hosting Mr. Grisham. It being such a last-minute cancellation, and the reason my host gave me was that you *changed your minds*?" She paused, then added, "I was just hoping to get a little clarification. As a business owner, it would help me to know if it was anything beyond just a change of heart." Orsa went quiet for a while as she absorbed what struck Larry as a lengthy response. At one point Orsa swiveled her chair back and forth and then away from Larry, to face out the window, then back.

"Okay," she finally said. "I see, I see." Larry could hear in his wife's voice a cosmic measure of restraint.

Her eyes narrowed as she thanked Paulette for her time and her honesty then she hung up.

Larry said, "What was it?"

Orsa blinked like a doll before saying, "She said it was the online reviews."

Larry's lip curled with surprise.

"Apparently," Orsa said, "the department head, the guy who planned Grisham's visit, got scared off after looking us up online. An hour or two ago the group was having cocktails back at the university reception hall following Grisham's speaking event, getting ready to head our way soon. The department head got out his phone to glance at our menu and ended up reading the online reviews. He got spooked. Didn't want to have an embarrassing situation where Grisham had a bad meal or a bad time."

Larry was stunned. "I didn't know anyone actually paid any attention to those things. I know you mentioned the other day that they've been bad lately. But bad enough to cancel? Where do they plan on feeding Grisham, I wonder, if not the best restaurant in town?"

"Apparently they decided to order in sushi from that new place, eat there on campus in the president's reception room where they've got that sunset view. Apparently Grisham likes sushi, and a view."

Larry could see Orsa's temperature rising and he decided he'd better scale back his own indignation to offer a voice of reason before Orsa acted rashly. "Let's take a minute," he said, "to digest. At least we know now that the Grisham reservation wasn't a hoax, so on the bright side, this isn't all some big conspiracy to ruin your life. Good riddance to the dishwasher, is what I say—I'd put money on him being your thief. Everything else, just a coincidence and a bad day. And the day's almost over now, isn't it? Start fresh tomorrow."

"This is far from over," Orsa said, "and I'm still inclined to think, far from a coincidence." The look in her eyes unsettled him.

"Be logical," Larry continued. "The steaks went missing during the last shift your dishwasher worked: Saturday night. His machinery supposedly malfunctions this afternoon, giving rise to him quitting right before a big VIP shift. So you and everybody else is rattled and screwed. It's got to be him that's acting out and acting alone."

"Well, I've got no great love for Willis," Orsa conceded. "And he does have a criminal record. The hire was a good deed. A second chance."

"A tiger can't change its stripes."

Orsa shook her head as she said, "But that doesn't square with the dishwasher unit crapping out before Willis was even in today. It would have been run many times prior to that—all morning, all afternoon, with no problem."

Orsa was quiet for a bit, mulling this over. Eventually she eased upright in her chair, turned to her computer, banged on her mouse a little bit and opened a browser window. "I'm going to have another look, refresh myself on the online reviews."

Larry watched his wife's steely jaw in profile as she pulled up the restaurant's Yelp page. "Newest review, just rolled in this morning. *Two stars, food was shit. Overdressed, wilted salad. Decent am Beyonce.*" She squinted at the screen, grappled for her reading glasses on their chain, put them on, and leaned closer. "Am Beyonce?"

"That's a singer," Larry informed her. "She's very popular."

"I know that," Orsa snapped. "Oh, I see, they meant *ambience*, I assume. What a moron. Who are these people?

James North. I'm looking him up on Facebook. By the way," Orsa said. "I keep meaning to ask you." She nodded toward her Facebook home page, which she had just pulled up. "Is your ex dying or something?"

"Diane? No, why? At least, I don't think so. Why?"

To prove her point, Orsa entered Diane's name into the Facebook search bar. She tilted the monitor to Larry's direction so he could see better.

He looked over the same collection of photos he'd seen many times before: mostly Diane's paintings, displayed crookedly and in poor lighting, and a few awkward selfies taken up the nose. He gazed at the pictures and shrugged. "And?"

Orsa looked back and forth incredulously between Larry and the screen. "Does this look like a healthy woman to you?"

"You're being cruel," Larry said.

"No, I'm not," Orsa said. "Just curious."

Larry figured that was true. Orsa had never been the least bit threatened by Diane. In fact, Orsa was the one who had encouraged Larry to send a Friend Request to Diane, back when he got on Facebook, and Orsa even sent one herself, reporting happily that Diane had swiftly "accepted" Orsa's friendship as though it meant something. Maybe it did. Larry didn't have a clue.

He said, "I'm sure Diane is fine. She's just old. Like me. Someday you will be, too, God willing."

"God willing!" Orsa snorted. "I could live to two hundred and not get old."

Larry figured that was true, too.

Orsa looked back to her screen. She typed madly for a

bit. “I can’t find any of the people who wrote these mean reviews. Who are they? Where are they?”

“They might not use their real names on the internet,” Larry pointed out. The internet depressed him, overwhelmed him. It was a place of no hope. It made things feel completely dire, and also devoid of all meaning.

Orsa clacked her fingernails against the keyboard. “This is making me feel like, well, I’ve half a mind to post a few choice reviews of some Grisham novels on Amazon or something. Give everybody a piece of my damn mind.”

Larry knew for a fact his wife hadn’t read any Grisham books. He said, “What on earth would that accomplish?”

Orsa shrugged. “It might feel good.”

THE HOST

THE PICTURE FROM THE HIKE THAT BYRON HAD posted on Facebook two days before ought to have been such a triumph and for a moment, it was.

Byron and Julia had been seeing one another/hooking up/hanging out—he meticulously avoided the terms *girlfriend* and even *dating*—for a number of months. Julia wasn't going to obsess over a label, or ask when she might meet his mother, who lived in town. She knew how quickly those conversations could throw cold water on a relationship, depending on the kind of guy you were dealing with. And what kind of a guy was Byron? Well, he was interesting. Or at least that was one of his favorite words: "interesting," followed closely by "uninteresting." In one of their very first conversations, just after Julia was hired at Aunt O's, Byron informed her that he was systematically replacing the "nice" people in his life with "interesting" ones. It seemed an odd and perhaps cruel thing to say. But several nights later at the end of a shift when Byron asked if Julia would like to continue their conversation at another venue, she found herself extremely flattered, taking this to mean that she was interesting versus nice—a distinction that suddenly felt thrilling and vital.

Julia had never had too hard a time getting the attention of a guy if she really wanted it (she was in college after all), but she'd never been pursued by an older guy whose culinary interests extended beyond beer and burgers, who would rather go to yoga or a museum than watch Sunday football, who smoked cigarettes in earnest, like he actually needed them, versus wanting or enjoying them. Byron loved books and hiking and photography and his dog. He had one photo album on Facebook and it was minimal but gorgeous, offering a curated selection of almost entirely landscape photos, and shots of his rescue, Ralphie, looking melancholy under a blanket. Several different girls, all breathtakingly beautiful, appeared in artful outdoor shots, but the most recent one of those was from over six months before.

Byron was attractive in a gloomy Jake Gyllenhaal kind of way. He lived in a small apartment with his best friend, a guy who delivered pizzas and knew a lot about movies. They had been best friends since childhood—both were townies—and roommates since freshman year of college. Byron didn't seem to have much of a social life beyond his roommate, but he had twice as many Facebook friends as Julia did, and his infrequent posts got tons of likes from tons of girls.

Even though Julia's classes, mostly electives, were a breeze and she had loads of free time during the day, when she and Byron hung out it was almost always late at night, after a shift. This was his preference because he had to prioritize his writing during the daytime hours. He wrote not at his apartment, where his roommate had evidently proven too distracting, but in his writing studio, a room elsewhere which, he explained, was free of clutter and disturbance. He was at work on a novel and a collection of poetry, and he and his roommate were brainstorming a screenplay. Several months into seeing one another, Byron had had a poem published in an online journal, which was accessible through a link on his Facebook page. Julia read the poem ten times and still didn't have a clue what it was about. Nevertheless, Byron's writing life was impressive to her—his studio, his solitude, his classified Moleskines, his rigid self-discipline—especially when compared to the aimless, fratty bozos she had dated before, and whom her suite-mates were all still torturing themselves over.

Sometimes Julia wished she and Byron could do what they typically did—drink wine and listen to music and eventually amble their way toward sex—at his studio rather than in his home which reeked of dog, cigarettes, and pizza, or hers, which was always heavily populated by her nosy suite-mates. She thought even if there were no bed available at Byron's studio, the privacy would be romantic and refreshing. But he never offered to take her there and she never wanted to ask for fear of desecrating his hallowed writing space or offending him with regard to his apartment.

Julia genuinely loved hearing Byron talk about art and philosophy and politics. He could really make her think. She started to dress more like him in subtle ways. She found herself less fulfilled by the superficial conversations she had with her peers. She found herself less likely to call her mother because she was hesitant to reveal too much about her new relationship, aware that her mother might express reservations. She was also less enthused by the prospect of teaching art history, which was her major, with teaching as her long-term plan up to this point. Instead, she wanted to cultivate her own art, and an artistic life. She wanted to be, and remain, interesting.

There had been a few awkward moments between them, one in particular when she mentioned that she was so inspired by him that she was thinking of trying to write a short story herself. She said she'd had a dream that sparked an idea, thinking Byron would find this intriguing and offer words of encouragement or advice. Instead, he frowned and said writing was not something a person should arrive at flippantly. He said, furthermore, that dreams never actually made for good material—something she would know if she had a better understanding of narrative. He added that she ought to become much more well-read before trying her hand.

Another awkward moment involved the Grisham reservation. After Julia took the reservation over the phone, word of it spread quickly among the staff. Someone had already told Byron about it by the time she next spoke to him. She said, "You must be awfully excited to see such a successful writer in person. Do you think you'll be his server? How many of his novels have you read?"

Byron stared at her like she had just produced a turd with her bare hand. He said, "I hope you're joking."

"I was," she assured him.

Byron said, "Orsa's gonna want Rhea on the table, which is just as well. You couldn't pay me a thousand bucks to *ohh* and *ahh* over a writer like that. Guy's a total hack."

Julia had read a few Grisham novels in high school, and thought they were really exciting. But now that she thought about it, she could recall several occasions when Byron had lamented the state of contemporary fiction—the depressing burden, as a writer, to meet readers' trivial and simple-minded demands such as "that something happen."

In any case, fortunately Byron seemed eager to move past this exchange, and recently things between him and Julia had felt easy and happy and more promising than ever.

The hike last weekend to the Yellow Ridge overlook had been a particular success in Julia's view, with perfect weather and foliage, and Byron in an unusually bright mood. As they hiked he breathlessly reported in vague terms a breakthrough he'd just made in the novel he was writing. He had brought his Moleskine, and took a few notes after periods of silence. They walked side by side, even when the trail was narrow and it would have been easier for one of them to fall a step ahead or behind. They stopped to look at some tracks in the mud that could have belonged to a bear cub, but then they thought, no, probably just a dog, even though pets weren't permitted on the trail. They admired the seafoam green moss that coated a fallen tree.

At the overlook Julia drank some water, did a deep stretch and enjoyed a couple different vantage points. When she turned back toward the trail, she found Byron facing the overlook but not looking at it, instead fiddling with his phone. Then, she was surprised to realize that he was taking her picture, cocking his head to get the right lighting and angle, tapping away. Julia stiffened and smiled, and he stopped. He didn't offer to show her the shots.

She had forgotten about the moment until this past Sunday, the day before yesterday, when she was startled to open Facebook to a shot of herself at the overlook, right there on Byron's timeline. Her heart raced and she was flooded with a warm and rapturous feeling. It was a stunning photo.

Here she was, lustrous and alive and in his company, for his many Facebook friends to see, the first girl to accompany his online presence in many months; the lone human in a sea of sunsets and dog portraits. Julia felt valid, proud, giddy. She allowed herself a closer look, to admire the composition of the shot.

In the photo, Julia was centered against the stone outcropping which reached her waist with the flamboyant autumnal mountain ridge sprawled out beyond her, the sky cloudless and cornflower blue, sunbeams illuminating her. She was partially facing Byron but oblivious to him and therefore striking the natural sort of pose that was impossible to achieve with effort: one of her hands resting on the stone, the other tucking hair behind an ear, her ankles crossed loosely. She looked sleek and serene—model-esque, even—just like the girls from his past. Her hair looked good, her outfit looked good, her skin and body looked good. Very good. In fact . . . Julia brought her phone closer to her face and squinted at it.

Was that . . . Oh, God. She felt a lurch. She stared at the photo closer to make sure. She zoomed in. Face. Waist.

Zoomed out. Zoomed in. Oh, God. It was so obvious. He hadn't even done a good job, if you were actually looking.

Every ounce of goodwill went hissing out of her in an instant and was replaced by abject humiliation and disbelief. *He hadn't even done a good job.*

Byron had photoshopped Julia's waist to look thinner than it actually was, smudging some extra foliage in on both sides to create a markedly tighter cinch. But this fabricated foliage met the stone wall wrong, and it blurred wrong against her shirt in the areas he had targeted, and where her shirt ought to have wrinkled instead it was as flat as spandex. As for her face, he had attempted to smooth out the acne scars that she was deeply self-conscious about. But her new flawless cheeks were waxy and weird, a partial shadow displaced, some strands of hair chopped off abruptly.

As Julia stared at the corrected version of herself, she was sure that never in her life had she felt such acute shame. She had a powerful urge to call her mother, who didn't even know Byron's name. Instead, she just kept staring at the photo and trying to understand herself.

Indeed, here she was, cured of her various imperfections, for all Byron's Facebook friends to see. All his friends, including the ones Julia shared—namely, the other restaurant staff members, who saw her and her face and her waist every day. All of them were on Facebook, even Orsa.

The picture had gone up on Sunday and she and Byron hadn't had any contact between then and today's shift. It was a little unusual to not at least exchange a few texts, but not unheard of. Especially if Byron had good momentum on one of his projects it could be a few days without hearing from him. But they were both always scheduled for Tuesdays, so Julia could generally look forward to seeing him at Aunt O's then. But this morning she'd found herself so sick at the thought of seeing Byron and the others that she had seriously contemplated calling out for the day, or even just quitting the job.

She needed the income, though. While Julia's parents were comfortably middle class—a teacher and a nurse—had provided her with a vehicle, and were helping with college, their financial support would end when she graduated in May. It wasn't that they couldn't (or wouldn't) help her out in a pinch, but they felt it was important for her to get herself established and create a life of her own. So Julia had gotten the job at Aunt O's in order to save money and also to function as a plan B if she didn't have either graduate school or a teaching job lined up come May. Thus far Julia's experience at Aunt O's had been fine except for Shannon, the pantry chef, who was always giving her crap, but everybody assured Julia this wasn't personal.

She had managed to gear herself up for today's shift when she remembered it was Grisham Day, so everybody would hopefully be so distracted by that that if in the past two days they had scrutinized or even God forbid discussed the edited picture among themselves, it would not be at the forefront of anyone's mind.

Once Julia was at the restaurant, it was very hard to say if the Grisham reservation was the only thing going on, because she had the distinct impression that people were avoiding her or at least avoiding her eyes. She had done her best to steer entirely clear of Byron, issuing merely a distant hand-wave then busying herself elsewhere, but she couldn't shake the feeling that something else was afoot. Others who were usually warm with her—Rhea and Kenzie, for example—didn't stop by the host stand for their typical debrief. Orsa inspected the dusting of the blinds and Windexing of the front doors which Julia had done, but didn't comment with either criticism or praise. Mired in her own private crisis about the photo, Julia became convinced that it was similarly on everyone else's minds; they had all seen it, she thought, and seen the edits. At best, they had silently and sympathetically drawn their own conclusions, at worst they had discussed it prior to her arrival and there had been a conferral of pity, a decision not to mention it.

When Julia learned that Willis had walked out, gone forever from the restaurant, she was tempted to follow suit. Instead, she powered through her humiliation with thoughts of the ice cream she would treat herself to tonight, no matter what it meant for her waist.

With some early walk-ins, happy hour traffic to the bar, the chaos surrounding the broken dishwasher and Willis's absence, and the pressure of both the pharma dinner and Grisham yet to arrive, Julia was distracted for several hours, and time passed painlessly.

When at six forty-five Julia took the call about the Grisham cancellation, she could have laughed or cried at the prospect of reporting back to Orsa. But to her surprise, she was able to pass off the unsavory task to Ant, the busser. Still, she knew that once the news had been relayed to Orsa, it was only a matter of time until Orsa stormed out of the office and to the host stand, to demand more information from Julia, or just to burn off steam.

To ready herself for this inevitable interaction, Julia

popped back to the kitchen a few minutes before seven, to grab a coffee.

As she entered the swinging door, she heard a shriek, "Glen! Oh my God!" followed by more. "Glen! Stop!" the first voice had been Shannon's; now this was Chef Oz: "Glen, your hand!"

Julia looked in the direction of the ruckus and saw Glen standing at his station, right hand still clutching a knife, left hand raised above a cutting board covered with cabbage, blood flowing from a finger.

Julia gasped.

Chef Oz clutched Glen by the shoulders, ushered him off the line and headed toward the sink. Blood splashed and splattered. It wasn't so much the volume of blood as it was the shock of the red against the stark white of Glen's apron.

Kenzie entered the kitchen, screamed, clapped a hand over her mouth.

"Get her the fuck out of here!" Chef Oz hollered over his shoulder, and Julia walked Kenzie to the swinging door, shushing her as she explained, "Always looks much worse than it really is."

Once Kenzie was out of the kitchen, Julia turned back. Shannon was shaking, still in her station. "He kept going," she said to no one in particular. She was wheezing and flapping her hands in a frenzied manner. "He was talking to me when it happened, looking at me while he chopped. He didn't stop until I screamed!"

Byron and Ant entered the kitchen together.

Byron said, "What the hell is going on in here? I could hear the screaming from the patio, where we have paying guests who are trying to enjoy a meal, in case everybody's forgotten."

When no one responded Byron scanned the room until he found Chef Oz and Glen at the sink. He edged closer for a look and staggered backward when he saw the blood. He steadied himself with a hand on the linen shelf. "Yikes," he murmured, looking for Julia, then at her, as though for strength. She'd never seen his face look wobbly like this before.

Ant the busser pushed by Byron to approach the sink. He made room for himself and assessed the injury.

Ant said, "Glen, how you doing, man?"

Glen did a half shrug. "Not bad, really."

Chef Oz said to Ant, "Who are you, the resident surgeon?"

Ant took Glen's forearm and gently guided it to a different angle where the water met the wound and he could get a better view. He leaned in close and said, "Easy, Glen, just look away if you need to. Here we are. Raise it higher, or actually, kneel here a little bit if you can, so it's above your heart, that'll help slow the bleeding. Chef, can you help, here? There we are. It's gonna be just fine. It's really not that bad." Ant reported over his shoulder, to the room: "It's gonna be okay, everybody. Fingertips bleed like hell. It's just a couple clean lacerations on his index and middle finger. Not very deep. We'll get a wrap and some pressure on it." He nodded toward the first aid kit on the wall. "He's gonna be just fine."

Julia was nearest to the first aid kit, and she grabbed it.

Chef Oz had stepped back from the sink. "Okay," he

said, "I guess Doogie Howser's got it under control. I'm gonna hop back on the line. We've got entrees out on the patio already, so we can take a sec to get ourselves sorted out. Since Grisham's not coming, we're through the worst of it all. Okay, Doc, you get Glen all taped up. Shannon, in the meantime, hop on up here for sides and sauce. Rhea, wherever she is, can plate desserts for you if we need her to. Looks like we're coming up on entrees on Five and Eleven—somebody grab Kenzie and tell her to get her shit together, we're gonna need her to run." He nodded toward Byron. "What about you, snowflake, you gonna make it? You're welcome for those entrees, by the way, on time and pretty as a picture. No, no, no need to thank us, sweating our asses off back here, down a man. Actually, down two now. No need to thank us. Give those pans a rinse, would you? Jesus Christ. Some help you are. Move, people, move."

Julia joined Ant and Glen at the sink, where she opened the first aid kit and fished around for gauze, bandaging tape, and ointment.

She said to Ant, "What else can I do?"

"I think we're good," Ant said to her, still holding Glen's arm up with one hand, and reaching for the first aid supplies with the other.

Julia returned to the host stand. She organized and stacked dinner menus, dessert menus, wine lists.

A few minutes later when Ant came by to peek at the floor plan, Julia said, "You were impressive in there."

Ant shrugged. "I've got four little brothers. I know my way around a flesh wound. You too, though—you were the only other one in there keeping their cool. Shannon was about to keel over, Chef can't stop yelling at people, and I still don't think Byron's recovered."

"My mom's an ER nurse," Julia said. "She was always explaining stuff to me, growing up. I usually found it interesting. When she stitched me up I liked to watch." A pang of sadness made Julia sway as she thought of her mother and her "World's Nicest Nurse" mug.

Rhea approached the host stand soon, announcing that she was bored now that Grisham wasn't coming. All but one of her other tables had cashed out.

Julia said, "Do you want walk-ins from here on out for the cash, or would you rather just close out Nine and be done with it?"

"I'd rather finish up," Rhea said. "Nine already has desserts. Kenzie should be fine to handle walk-ins though I doubt you'll get many." She shoved a bobby pin farther into her tight bun and regarded Julia. "Hey, babe, you okay?"

Before Julia answered, Rhea lowered her voice to add: "None of us really think you did it, by the way."

Julia frowned. "Did what?" It was a moment before she realized what Rhea might be referring to. Julia hadn't even considered the possibility that people might think she had edited the picture for Byron to post. Was it less of a public travesty if people believed she had done the edits herself?

Rhea gave her a strange look. "The steaks, obviously. Orsa talked to you, right?"

Julia said, "What steaks?"

"The missing—oh, God. Well, don't tell her I told you, I thought she was going to pull you aside hours ago, she must have changed her mind. Some steaks went missing over the weekend," Rhea explained, "and you were on the short list of suspects that she was going to talk to. You seemed off your game today. I figured that was why."

Julia was so taken aback she laughed. "Orsa thinks I stole steaks?"

"I know. Like I said, none of the rest of us really think it was you."

"None of who?"

"The servers. I guess I don't know what the kitchen thinks. But Kenzie and Byron and me all think Shannon did it." She paused. "Wait. Byron didn't give you a heads-up? That's weird, I would've thought, even though Orsa told us not to say anything to anybody . . . I guess I would've thought he'd say something to you, since you two are . . ."

Julia glanced at Rhea, then away. She was trying to reveal nothing, feel nothing, because she desperately did not want to cry at work. But her face must have betrayed her because Rhea touched her arm gently and said, "Oh no. He did it to you, too, didn't he?"

"He did . . ." Julia paused. Was Rhea talking about the edited photo? If she had seen it, surely she wouldn't be posing this as a question. Julia didn't want to launch into the Facebook thing if that was not what Rhea was referring to, so she didn't say anything else.

Rhea seemed to take her expression as an affirmative and said, "Julia, I'm sorry. He's notorious. Don't worry. You're not the first. We've all seen it happen to other girls before you."

Once again Julia did not speak, hoping that Rhea would carry on, which she did. "We wanted to warn you about him," Rhea said, "but as always he got his hooks in first before any of us had the chance to become your friend. And once he's got his sights set . . . he gets so territorial, you know. Always snagging the seat next to you during your shiftie, always lurking around the host stand so no one else has the chance to chat to you, always whisking you off to hang out after the shift so you won't go to McCabb's with us for a nightcap . . . Just, basically, laying claim. Making sure you don't actually ever hang out with anyone other than him."

Julia's head was spinning. "Is that what you meant about *other girls . . .*"

"Well," Rhea hesitated. "I was referring to what always eventually happens with Byron and girls. We've seen it plenty of times before. The host before Kenzie, a bartender from France, this server who was in grad school, now I can't even remember her name . . . I could swear there are more . . . And it always ends the same."

"How does it end?" Julia murmured. She hated to seem needy or naive but had to know.

"He loses interest," Rhea said. She looked at Julia. "I don't mean to assume," she said. "I just figured. I'm sorry."

"It's okay," Julia said. She thought and thought and couldn't decide if Byron losing interest in her would be better or worse than what had happened with the photo. Or maybe, it occurred to her, what happened with the photo was a form of lost, or waning, interest. Because come to think of it, she didn't think there was ever more than one picture of the same girl on his Facebook.

Julia felt sick with stupidity and self-contempt as she reflected on the many ways she had recast herself in the hopes of maintaining his interest. *Show me exactly what you want*, she had implored not with these words but with everything else. *Don't worry about the dimensions of the box, I'll make sure I fit.*

"Don't get me wrong," Rhea said. "I get along with Byron just fine. He can be a tool but I have no real issue with anything he's ever done to me personally. He's just a jerk to the girls he dates. A playboy. I've never quite understood that. He's not my type, I guess. Doesn't matter. This might cheer you up, though," Rhea offered. "It's a secret. I assume he's told you about his writing studio, where he spends all his daytime hours?"

Julia nodded.

"A while back, his mom came here with one of her friends for a cocktail at the bar, and Darius overheard his mom talking about him to her friend." Rhea paused. "Stop me if you already know this . . . Have you ever met his mom?"

Julia shook her head.

"Apparently," Rhea continued, "his mom was crowing to her friend about what an amazing guy Byron is, working evenings and weekends here at the best restaurant in town, to support himself while he works on all of these writing projects. She's just totally agog about it, going on and on. And then she mentions to her friend that she's so glad she's been able to keep his childhood bedroom as his space—that it's where he does all his writing. So she still gets to see him almost every day even though he's usually hard at work."

Julia's eyes popped wide. "His writing studio is his childhood bedroom in his parents' house?"

Rhea snickered. "Apparently she makes him bologna sandwiches for lunch just like she did when he was a kid."

"Oh my God." Julia tried to laugh but couldn't.

Rhea said, "I know. It's so sad and stupid. I don't think anybody knows except Darius and me. When Darius told me we had a good chuckle then realized we couldn't tell anybody else or Byron would literally get laughed out of the building." Rhea lowered her voice as Ant approached the host stand. "Can you imagine if Chef Oz knew? So you really can't say anything. Also because Byron . . . Well, I'll put it this way . . . I really don't want him to know I'm blabbing about him. It's in my best interests not to piss off Byron." Julia was tempted to ask more about this but Rhea turned abruptly to Ant. "What's up, kid?"

"Nine just snagged me," he said. "They're ready for the bill. Don't even want to see dessert menus."

"Good," Rhea said. "Good riddance." She reached into her apron for her black vinyl book, glanced at their ticket, put it back. "How's Glen doing back there, by the way?"

Ant said, "All wrapped up and back on the line. I'll check it and change the dressing a little later, probably once desserts are out to the patio. Come to think of it, he might have a hard time dealing with the dressing on his own, seeing as it's a hand. I wonder if he's got anyone to help him."

Rhea said, "Thank God you were here, I'm not kidding, Ant. Who knew you'd be the one to lead us through the storm?"

"Julia would've been just fine stepping in," Ant said. "Her mom's an ER nurse, you know."

"I didn't know," Rhea said. She turned to Julia. "Did she send you to school in plastic wrap? I had a friend growing up whose dad was an ER doc. She had ten times more rules than the rest of us."

"Nah," Julia said. "I didn't grow up with a bunch of extra rules. Just some extra horror stories."

"That's fair," Rhea said. "It's a crapshoot, anyhow. That friend ended up blind in one eye from a foul ball."

THERE WERE CERTAIN activities Julia's ER nurse mom had always warned Julia about: biking without a helmet, playing with fire, jumping into a body of water without knowledge of its depth. Stuff that seemed so obviously dangerous, so certain to end in injury, that Julia wouldn't have done it anyway. Her mother had not offered explicit advice on dating, but Julia realized now, well, yes, she probably had—it just always seemed so obvious that Julia hadn't bothered to take it seriously.

Well, and anyway, as much as Julia loved her mom, she wasn't always right about everything. For instance back when Julia was in the eighth grade, waking an hour early every day in order to work painstakingly with primer, concealer, setting powder, and foundation to cover her pimples, and then a few years later when it was the same morning schedule and similar products—not to cover the pimples anymore but to cover the scars left by them—Julia's mother issued blatant falsehoods, one after another, such as: *You're beautiful.* And *No one else even sees them.*

AFTER ANT LEFT the host stand, Julia and Rhea both laughed a little bit about Byron's writing studio. But the laughter began to feel bad as soon as Rhea had left Julia's side, to go drop the bill on Nine.

Suddenly, Julia felt deeply, inordinately sad. Not, she realized, for Byron nor even for herself, but for the one person in the world who would be even more pained than her by the edited picture, and the one person who would be even more pained than Byron to witness the mockery of his coworkers over the bologna sandwiches. Julia felt an ancient and incontrovertible ache as her heart broke for the mothers, both of them and all of them, for the enormity of their love, and the grandiosity of their delusions.

THE BARTENDER

EARLIER IN THE SHIFT DARIUS HAD LEARNED from Rhea that Grisham wasn't coming, and she seemed equally glad to be relieved of the burden and disappointed by the loss of income. For his part, Darius was thrilled. He'd been running his ass off for the first two hours of the shift, trying to relieve the dish load on the kitchen by washing and polishing as many racks in the bar as he could. On top of this, a few of the doctors on the patio were drinking the most labor-intensive cocktails—a Ramos gin fizz, a Sazerac, an espresso martini—and some bar regulars, oblivious to Darius's stress, wouldn't shut up about fantasy football, haranguing him for his opinion. All of his food took ages. He was vaguely aware of some drama—the whole dishwasher debacle, Glen's injury, and whispers about a potential theft over the weekend—but didn't have time to speculate or dwell on any of it. The rush ended as abruptly as it started, though. After the Grisham cancellation there was only one more reservation, a deuce that went to Kenzie, and the bar cleared out a few minutes before eight.

Rhea sat down for her shiftie at eight o'clock, which was a rarity. She was typically the last to finish up and close out and was often too exhausted and eager to leave to enjoy a drink. Darius was happy for her company at the bar when she was in the right mood.

After her shiftie, Rhea ordered a Malbec, and halfway through that, she confided in Darius about the stolen steaks. "Twenty-two, disappeared after Saturday's shift," she said. She assured him he was not on the short list of suspects.

"Obviously," he said. "I've got access to the drawer every single night. If I was gonna make off with anything it'd be cash. And a lot of it. But how did Orsa reach that conclusion?"

"Surveillance footage from the bank of people leaving the building. Anybody without a bag big enough for that haul is off the list."

Darius was tempted to pry more, but Rhea did not offer up further information and instead disappeared into her phone for a while.

Eventually she ordered another Malbec. "I'm not lingering to try to work up the courage to make a pass at you," she clarified. "Disappointing, I know. I'm here at Orsa's request. She wants to confer about something."

"The missing steaks?"

"I assume so. I wasn't supposed to say anything to anybody. Don't let on that I did."

"Don't leave me totally in the dark. Who are the suspects? The stakes are high, huh? Somebody here's got beef?"

Rhea waved her hands in the air. "Please stop." She glanced around and lowered her voice. "We're all leaning toward Shannon."

Darius agreed, "She does have the most beef."

Ant came back to the bar at eight thirty to report that desserts were down on the pharma dinner and entrees were cleared on Kenzie's last two tables in the place.

Hypothetically, Julia would seat walk-ins in the dining room for another half hour, but on a weeknight, anything after eight thirty was rare. The bar served drinks and desserts until ten, but late bar traffic was also uncommon on a Tuesday.

Darius said, "How are things in the kitchen?"

Ant said, "Everybody's spent but happy now that the end's in sight."

Rhea piped up, "I would've come back to help with dishes, team player that I am, but it seemed like everything was under control."

"All good," Ant said. "Now that desserts are out on the patio, Shannon and Glen were able to both hop off the line and get us all caught up on dish."

Rhea said, "The repair guy never showed up, I guess."

"He called Chef Oz half an hour ago," Ant said. "Apparently he got hung up on a job out in Quartersburg. Oz told him not to bother tonight. We'll be his first call tomorrow morning." With a grin, Ant added, "Larry's been back there on his hands and knees for a while, though."

Rhea said, "So we're officially doomed."

Darius looked at the clock. He wondered if the drama surrounding the missing steaks and the missing Grisham and the dishwasher debacle would mean more staff drinks than usual, or fewer. After a terrible shift, it could always go either way.

Soon, Orsa showed up and took a seat next to Rhea. She set a yellow legal notepad and some other papers on the bar. "Thanks for waiting around," she said to Rhea.

Darius twirled a pen. "What'll it be, boss?"

"Surprise me," Orsa said.

Darius truly hated when she said this. It was clear she was not someone who ever actually wanted to be surprised.

He grabbed a bottle from behind him and waggled it. "Salesgirl for Baylor's was in earlier, left this sample for us."

"What is it?"

Darius read the label: "Vanilla-Honey Pear Cider."

Orsa made a face. "Gimme a Tanqueray tonic. Make it a double, on the double."

"Yes, ma'am."

Darius retrieved a chilled highball glass and filled it nearly to the top with ice. He measured a double shot of gin with his jigger, poured, and stirred carefully around the edge with his swivel bar spoon to preserve the ice. He topped off with tonic water and stirred again. He garnished with a slice of lime and placed it on a cocktail napkin before Orsa. It was a classic stunner of a drink that he could appreciate for its sparkle and purity even though he personally didn't care for gin.

Orsa took an approving sip then focused her attention to Rhea.

Darius turned to face the wall of bottles, behind which

was a mirror that offered him a view of his bar guests even with his back turned to them. He began to methodically wipe down each bottle with a rag, a mindless task that permitted him to eavesdrop. Like all good bartenders, Darius had mastered the two most important aspects of his job: pretending he was listening when he was not listening, and pretending he was not listening when he was.

Orsa was shuffling her papers and saying to Rhea, "I printed all the negative reviews out here and I've been mulling them over for the past hour. Taking a closer look since apparently they were enough to scare off the Grisham handlers. They *are* bad. Stupid people with stupid opinions. I don't actually feel like getting into it now. The reviews don't really relate to you anyway, they're almost entirely about the food. It's been an onslaught, this past month. You're on the floor every night. Are the reviews right? Are we sending out slop?"

Rhea said, "From my view things have been solid. No more complaints on the floor lately, than before. Obviously people are getting more and more *online* in general. Everybody shouting into the void. But here, let me take a quick look at those."

Darius wiped the neck of a Midori bottle and used his thumb to flatten the curled corner of its black label.

Before any more words were exchanged behind him, Orsa flagged Darius down for a limoncello. "One for Rhea, too. We've been through it."

Darius poured and set before them two tiny glasses of the pale-yellow liquid, the smell of which always made him salivate even though he didn't actually care for the taste.

It was quiet as they sipped, and when Darius next

turned to face them, Rhea was tapping the papers before her with a curious expression. She said, "You know, looking at these, it occurs to me—"

"Not a moment's peace," Orsa interrupted her, and Darius turned to see that Larry was approaching. He wore latex gloves and a streaked apron over a very yellow sweater.

Darius said, "Hey, Lare, you want another—"

Larry cut him off with a wave of his hand and addressed Orsa: "You're never going to believe it."

"You fixed it?" Orsa said. "You're right—I don't believe it."

"I found the problem."

"But you didn't fix it."

"A clogged disposal tripped the breaker," Larry said. "Automatic defense mechanism so it doesn't back up. The blades got overworked and the whole thing shut itself down. As soon as I could see the power setting was tripped, I got in there, under the drain, to remove the upper grinding chamber and get into the connector line. Sure enough, it was a clog in the disposal. The lower chamber, that's why Oz wasn't able to get in there with his hand. Care to venture a guess as to the source of the clog?"

Orsa blinked, then gasped. "Steak."

"You got it."

Rhea's mouth gaped open.

Larry said, "Tendon and tissue, all tangled and mangled and bloody. By the looks of it I think it's probably only one steak, two or three at most. But you wouldn't believe the mess."

Rhea said, "So this means, whoever did it—"

"What this means," Orsa interrupted, "is that now we know who did it, beyond a shadow of a doubt."

"You mean . . ." Rhea said. She paused. "Well, what do you mean?"

"Rhea," Orsa said, "you know the staff as well as I do. There's only one person here that's deranged enough to shove a steak down the damn disposal."

"You mean Shannon," Rhea confirmed.

"We'll check inventory to know for sure, but I assume this afternoon, Shannon grabbed one of the replacements Larry picked up, shoved it down there to screw us all right before the big shift." Orsa slammed the rest of her limoncello and rose from her barstool.

Larry said, "Hon, maybe—"

"Nah, this can't wait," Orsa said. "Let them all hear me roar." She teetered unsteadily off her barstool.

Rhea made big eyes at Darius and rose to follow Orsa.

"Oh, God," Larry said. "I can't be there for this. I'll be in the office." To Darius, he said, "Have somebody come get me if things take a turn."

Darius wasn't sure what sort of a turn would constitute retrieving Larry but he agreed.

Then Darius did not wait long before making his own way back to the kitchen. Usually the drama bored him, but this was a new level.

He carried a full rack of polished glassware as this would justify his presence in the kitchen if anyone gave him a look, but it turned out he didn't need an excuse because by the time he got back there Orsa was already going off and all eyes were on her.

Chef Oz was at the grill, wire brush in hand. Glen was spreading cellophane over the tips of the sauce bottles. Shannon was updating masking tape labels at the ice cream freezer. Byron was polishing silver, Kenzie was polishing glassware, Julia was refilling salt into the tiny stainless-steel canisters for resets.

Orsa was saying, "Who are we missing? Who's here now, but not *here* now?" She stared around the room.

Rhea offered, "Just Ant, right? He's probably out on resets."

Byron said, "Affirmative. Ant just helped me break down the patio."

Orsa said, "Okay—he doesn't need to be here. I assume the rest of you are aware Larry's been hard at work on the dishwasher. Anyone care to take a guess at what he found stuffed into the disposal, that made the whole thing shut down, resulting in all of you becoming dishwashers for the night?"

They looked around at each other, and Shannon, who was closest to the dishwasher, took a step closer to peer underneath it, at the pile of tools and five-gallon bucket.

"Steak!" Orsa exploded. "Some psychopath in this very room shoved a stolen rib eye down the disposal! I imagine my HR department would recommend I hold meetings in private, but you all suffered on account of this, so you all deserve the truth and an apology, from the horse's mouth." She blinked as she looked around the room, her gaze eventually settling on Shannon. "It's one thing to lash out at me," Orsa said, "but to put all the rest of your colleagues through this . . ."

Shannon's mouth dropped. "I would never," she said. "And when we talked earlier, you said you had changed your mind and didn't actually think it was me. You said—"

"Things have changed," Orsa interrupted her. "New evidence has been presented."

Shannon demanded, "Such as . . ."

"I'm not going to spell it all out," Orsa said.

It was quiet for a moment.

From the other side of the kitchen, Chef Oz spoke evenly. "I don't have a dog in this fight, but I think it bears pointing out, as it relates to your list of suspects from earlier, it seems probable that the steaks never left the building. I can do a quick count now to see if the one in the disposal was snagged from the new stash today, but regardless, I think maybe it wasn't safe to assume that they were ever taken out of here on Saturday."

Orsa shook her head vehemently. "Between Danny, Larry, and me, we've searched this place top to bottom. Saturday's missing steaks are *not here*. They left the building Saturday. I'm sure of it."

Chef Oz said, "Bear with me. If we just *imagine* that the steaks didn't leave the building, then that opens up the possibility of everybody you initially crossed off your list on account of the parking lot footage. Like, say, our all-star servers." Chef Oz tipped his head in the direction of Kenzie and Byron who stood next to each other.

Orsa insisted, "*I told you*, the building's been searched top to bottom, and—"

Kenzie broke in, with screeching laughter, "Are you serious, Chef? You guys know how I am about raw meat. And, *stealing*, really? I don't need—or want—two steaks, much less twenty. And I don't have issues with anyone here. Except you," she pointed at Oz, "because you're mean to me. But other than that, I have nothing to say to anyone here, at all. No feelings, good or bad. I'm literally just biding my time here. I literally don't care about this place *at all*."

"Lovely," Chef Oz remarked.

Byron said, "She is right, though—she doesn't."

Chef Oz turned back to Kenzie, tapping his lip. "Come to think of it, haven't we been seeing more of you lately? I overheard you talking schedule with Rhea a while back, reminding her you're *wide-open*. I didn't think anything of it at the time. But since when are you hard up?"

"I'm always wide-open in the evening," Kenzie said. "I'm a college student."

"But since when do you want extra shifts?" Chef Oz said. "I always thought you worked the bare minimum to keep yourself employed, per the terms of your family agreement. You hurting for cash?"

Kenzie didn't respond but her eyes flicked toward Rhea.

Rhea looked back and forth between Chef Oz and Kenzie a few times then said to Kenzie, "You might as well tell them. He's not going to let it go."

Oz said, "Tell us what?"

Kenzie protested, "It's none of their business, Rhea. I didn't take the stupid steaks. That's all anyone needs to know."

Oz demanded, "Tell us what?"

When Kenzie didn't respond, Rhea said to her, "It's going to come out one way or another."

Byron was looking at Kenzie. "You *have* been working extra shifts lately," he noted curiously. "And offering to take the late tables nobody else wants."

Kenzie shifted and squirmed, her face gone deep red.

Rhea said to the room. "You're right, Kenzie asked me to put her on extra shifts a month or two ago and throw her on late tables. Okay? It's her personal business why." Rhea turned to Kenzie. "Although, you really shouldn't be embarrassed about it. In fact, people would probably like you a lot better if they knew the truth. But it's up to—"

"Hoo boy," Chef Oz cut in, swirling his hands with intrigue. "This sounds delicious. Did Daddy cut you off?"

Rhea told him to shut up.

Orsa said, "Well now *I've* got to know."

Chef Oz said, "What'd you do to piss off your old man enough to cut off your allowance? One too many shopping sprees at Victoria's Secret?"

Kenzie scowled.

Rhea said to her, "Babe, you should really just explain so we can move past it."

Kenzie puffed out a hot, ragged breath and said to Oz, "Okay, you jerk, you actual ass, if you must know, my dad was laid off a couple months ago."

"Oh." Chef Oz's posture changed.

Orsa said, "Wasn't he with a big bank?"

Kenzie nodded. "Wave of layoffs after another bad quarter. It wasn't personal. We're fine. It's not like we're desperate. My parents just asked me . . . Well, it's not that they *needed* me to pitch in more, and it's just like, temporary, but between tuition, and the membership dues for sorority . . ." Her voice trailed off, then returned strong to reiterate: "It's temporary. And it's not like we're poor. It's not like we're struggling."

Orsa said, "My friend's husband who was with a big bank got laid off over a year ago and he's still looking."

Shannon said, "If you need help applying for food stamps, I've got you."

Kenzie blinked. "I genuinely do not know if you're joking."

Chef Oz spoke genially to Kenzie, "Rhea was right. I do like you more now." He turned to address Rhea. "And I admire your discretion but I have to say, in light of the theft, you didn't think this was relevant? Orsa asked us specifically if anyone was having money trouble. Struggling."

Kenzie said, "I just told you, I'm not struggling."

Orsa affirmed, "That is true though, Rhea. I did ask for that information."

Rhea said to Orsa, "You ruled Kenzie out right away on account of the video footage. Kenzie had no way to get the steaks out, with just her little purse. So I figured her personal finances were irrelevant."

Orsa said, "I suppose you're right." To Kenzie, she said, "Sorry about your dad."

Byron, who was standing near to Kenzie, said, "Me too." He put a hand on her shoulder. "I had no idea. You didn't think you could say anything to me?"

"Um," Kenzie said, making a face. ". . . No."

Byron retracted his hand. "I thought we were pals."

Kenzie said, "I didn't want it showing up in your book."

Byron looked taken aback, but before he could respond, Chef Oz piped up. "Speaking of that," he said to Byron, "how *is* your novel coming?"

Byron squinted.

Orsa said, "What novel again? The one you guys were talking about earlier?"

Chef Oz answered, "The one he's writing about all of

us." Pointedly, to Byron, he said, "I don't blame Kenzie for not wanting to divulge any personal information to you."

Byron scoffed, "You don't have a clue what I write about."

Chef Oz demanded, "So it's *not* a novel about all of us? Go ahead, get out your little Moleskine and prove it. I bet it's chock-full of material from today."

Rhea said, "You've seen inside one of Byron's Moleskines? He doesn't let anybody near those things."

Chef Oz said, "No, I haven't read it, but I know how he looks at me. At all of us. And apparently he tells Edgar what he's writing about and tries to get information out of Edgar about all of us—probably assumes Edgar's safe since he's not part of our evening crew—but that shit gets back to me."

Byron said, "You have no clue what I think about anybody. Neither does Edgar. I just happen to like chatting with the guy. But while we're on the topic of my personal opinions . . ." He turned to Orsa. "Just curious, on what basis was Chef ruled out as a suspect?"

Orsa scratched her head. "I can't remember right now. But I'm sure I had a good reason."

"Well," Chef Oz said, "if anyone wants my opinion, here it is: Our writer-in-residence took the steaks right before Grisham Day to gin up some drama, observe the fallout, and have an actual plot for his book."

Byron snorted. When no one jumped in right away to defend him or disagree with the theory, he rationalized, "First off, I would never write a *mystery*. I'm not that desperate. I'm not a hack. Secondly, I don't know why you're so shocked by the idea that a writer might draw from the people they see every—"

"It's theft!" Chef Oz interrupted. "It's—"

"Writers borrow from people's real lives all the time, dude. Get over it."

"Borrow?!" Chef Oz demanded. "When and how exactly do you plan on returning what you take?"

"If you're so paranoid about how you might appear in someone's story"—Byron spoke coolly—"maybe you should think about changing the way—"

Orsa interrupted, "Stop, you two. This makes my head hurt and has nothing to do with steaks anyway. Rhea . . ." She turned to her. "You know the most about everyone and everything. People"—she nodded in Kenzie's direction—"confide in you. You know this place and this staff inside and out. Look around this room, at these people and the evidence. What do *you* think?"

Rhea was holding the printed-out Yelp reviews Orsa had brought to her at the bar. She lifted them into the air. "I think," Rhea announced, "that someone's got it out for Shannon. First the reviews, then—"

"Forget I asked," Orsa said.

"Hear me out," Rhea said. "Almost every review that's come in in the last month singles out something that came from Shannon—salad or dessert plating. When you look at them all together, it's just too much, too many, too one-sided for them to be legitimate, in my opinion. And you said yourself that you couldn't find any other public reviews any of these supposed guests posted, and no online presence for any of them at all. It reeks of someone fabricating reviews to try to take down Shannon. And with the steaks, I mean, look. We all know Shannon has her issues with this place. The Julia hire, et cetera. Shannon's the only one who gripes openly. We all know she's pissy, maybe vindictive, even. And we all know she carries that big duffel and a cooler in and out every single day, she always has a full locker, plenty of room to hide things and haul things—the appearance of guilt, is what I mean. Furthermore, we all know if anybody in here is going to lose their temper over getting falsely accused, if anybody in here is going to get riled enough to, say, get themselves fired over an accusation alone, it's Shannon." Rhea turned back to Orsa. "So, that's what I think. Somebody wrote all these fake reviews, and when nothing came of it, when Shannon's job wasn't jeopardized over that, they decided to frame her for theft."

"Whoa." Chef Oz broke a stunned silence. "Whoa, Rhea."

Rhea continued, "But what I can't figure out, is *who.* I mean, Chef, you're the one who has conflict with pretty much everybody here, at one point or another. You're the obvious asshole. But as far as I can tell"—she pointed back and forth between Oz and Shannon—"you two actually get along; Shannon's the one person on staff who you actually like."

"That is true," Chef Oz said. "And Glennie. I do like Glennie."

Glen, who had been silent and noncommittal thus far, nodded appreciatively. Rhea said, "Glen, you're back here in the middle of things and working right next to Shannon all the time. What do you think? Who's got it out for her?"

Glen was quiet for a bit then looked around the room and said simply, "I can't imagine any of you doing any of this. I really can't."

Rhea sighed. She turned toward Julia, who looked

plainly miserable. "Shannon's got it out for you," Rhea said, "because you stepped into the front of house spot she wanted, but do *you* have it out for *her*?"

Everyone turned to Julia, who said, "No, I really don't."

Darius glanced at Shannon, whose fists were dug into her waist, and she finally spoke up now, addressing Julia directly. She said, "It's not like I'm *cruel* to you."

Julia spoke softly, "No, you're not, and I've never taken it personally. I would never try to sabotage you, Shannon, I swear to God it wasn't me."

Orsa shook her head back and forth. To Julia she said, "But you were carrying that big bag when you left Saturday night. I saw it on the footage. I don't recall you carrying a bag that big before."

Julia said, "I bring my duffel any time I come straight from the gym. Which isn't that often. But sometimes I work out, shower at the gym and come straight here." Her voice had shrunk to a whisper. "You guys." Julia looked around the kitchen. "I wouldn't do this."

"Can you guys lay off her?" Byron piped up. "She really wouldn't."

Rhea said to Shannon, "Do *you* have any theories? Anybody else here who you think has it out for you?"

Shannon put her hands out before her in a gesture of exasperated disbelief. "I know I'm not the nicest person on staff but I don't think I've done anything to anyone here that would make them want to get me fired; in this job market, knowing I'm a single mom. Fired or worse. Arrested, I mean. I know I can be a bitch but come on."

Rhea looked around the room again and settled her gaze on Byron. "About those Moleskines," she said. "If you've got nothing to hide, why don't you let me take a look in that one you've got in your apron right now?"

Byron snorted.

"I'm serious," Rhea said. "We've been working together, how many years? All this time you're hunched over your little books, scribbling away, and you've never once let me see. That one time you dropped one in the server station you practically broke your neck making sure you got to it before I could."

"How many different ways do I have to tell you people it's none of your business?" Byron insisted. "And what would you be looking for anyway?"

"Could be anything," Rhea said. "Maybe some harsh words about Shannon. Eh? If you didn't drum up all this drama, prove Chef Oz wrong. Prove you've got nothing mean to say about any of us, and nothing to hide." She edged closer to him and held her hand out expectantly.

"Wow." Byron stepped back from her and placed both hands over the pocket where his Moleskine and server book lived. "You can pry it out of my dead hands. Wow," he said again. "*Rhea.* Rhea, Rhea, Rhea. You of all people. Thought you and me were tight. I've always had your back, you know." He gave her a knowing look, forehead tipped her way. "You know what I'm talking about."

Rhea said, "Whee! Here we go, everybody. Here it comes."

"You brought this on yourself, lady," Byron spoke ruefully. "Pushing me on the Moleskine thing. You know I never would've said a word about it if you hadn't pushed me."

Chef Oz looked back and forth between them. "Said a word about *what*?"

Rhea said stridently to Byron, "Go ahead, you asshole. Say it. Dare you. Tell everyone. What do I care?"

Orsa's head jerked back and forth. "What are you guys talking about?"

"Go ahead, Byron," Rhea said again, louder. "Say it. You gave me your word that you wouldn't. Now you're just proving you're willing to say anything, betray anyone, to distract people and confuse things. So go on then, tell the room."

Byron had fallen silent, and he looked away from her.

Chef Oz said to him, "Clearly you have something on Rhea. Spit it out. She's practically begging."

When Byron remained silent, Rhea threw her hands in the air. "Oh, you're not going to now? It was just an empty threat? You coward. You prick." She looked around the room. "It's got nothing to do with the steaks, by the way, in case anybody's worried about that. It's old news."

Chef Oz said, "We're airing it all out today. So what's he got on you, Rhea? You know it's going to come out—if not here and now, then in his book."

Rhea snorted. "You're probably right. Well then. We're all friends here, right? I haven't broken the law. I haven't stolen from the restaurant."

Byron broke in. "Rhea, you really don't have to—I wasn't actually going to—"

"No, no." She waved her index finger. "Chef Oz is right. The last person in the world I want having any power over me, carrying a secret of mine, is you. Might as well just get it all out now." She looked at the others in the room. "If you all want to know what Byron knows, here it is: Every six months or so, I send a pair of my work socks to a man in Mishawaka."

There was a brief silence then confused laughter. Chef Oz was the loudest. He cupped a hand around his ear. "Sorry, ma'am. What did you say? You send your socks to *a man in Mishawaka*?"

Rhea explained: "A couple years ago I served a table in here, some rich businessmen traveling through. Idiots. Drunk. Lewd. And I gave it right back to them. Didn't take their crap. Sassed them back, scolded them, told them to behave. Well, apparently one of those guys has a bit of a *thing* about women telling him to behave."

Kenzie shrieked.

Rhea continued, "And apparently he has some other . . . *things* too. When he got up to use the bathroom, his buddies told me he'd taken a liking to me and my tone, and that it was his birthday, and they offered me a hundred bucks to put my dirty work socks in a to-go bag and send it with them."

There was another brief silence, then more laughter and a few whistles.

Orsa was the only one not laughing. She wore a traumatized grimace.

Chef Oz said, "You said *Mishawaka*?"

"That's where he lives," Rhea explained. "He found me on Facebook after that night and every now and then, couple times a year, he sends me a message and asks me to mail him a pair of my oldest work socks, then he PayPals me a hundred bucks. Plus shipping." She looked at Orsa. "Sorry you had to hear this. But I don't think it's wrong, technically."

Kenzie was cracking up. "Does your boyfriend know?"

Rhea nodded. "Approves, heartily. Dies laughing every time I get the message. Anybody else have questions? Anything at all." She looked at Chef Oz. "I suppose you've got all sorts of thoughts on this, Cosimo."

Chef Oz scratched his nose. "Speechless. I'm just thinking back on all the times you've told me to *shut up* and *behave* . . . all this time, I've been getting that treatment for free?"

Rhea laughed.

"I'm honored," Chef Oz said. "So, how—why—does Byron know about this?"

"I stuck around after my shiftie one night, maybe a year or two ago, had a few too many, got into a funny mood and spilled my guts about it to Byron, who just happened to be at the bar sitting next to me. We had a good laugh. He was nice about it. He promised he'd never tell. *Promised.*" She turned to Byron. "So now we know how good his word is."

"Give me a break," Byron said. "You're the one who told everybody just now, not me. I wasn't going to. And I didn't think it was that big of a deal. I never actually thought I was the only one who knew." He nodded toward Darius. "I mean, Darius hears everything in the bar. Right? I'm sure he overheard your whole socks story that night. It's not like you were whispering."

Rhea turned to Darius, who confirmed, "Yeah, I did hear it."

Rhea turned back to Byron. "Fair enough. But, gentleman that he is, Darius never mentioned it or held it over my head. He would never blackmail a friend."

Darius put his hands out in front of him. "The lady is right," he said.

Orsa said loudly: "If we can stop talking about the socks? For the love of God! I don't ever want to think about that again. Have we all forgotten about my stolen steaks? Please! Please! Where were we with *that*?"

Rhea said, "We were establishing that it is most likely someone who has a grudge against Shannon and is trying to frame her."

Orsa said, "But we weren't getting anywhere with that."

Darius looked at everyone in the room. Considering what had just occurred, the whys and hows of Rhea's disclosure, and the cruelty of the intended sabotage of Shannon—a single mom, as she had pointed out, in a tough job market—Darius found himself unable to hold his silence any longer. He said, "I know someone who might have a grudge against Shannon."

Everyone looked at him.

Orsa demanded, "Well, who? Who?!"

Darius said, "Byron."

"Oh God." Byron made a crazed expression. "Let me try to keep up. I'm a suspect, then I'm not, then I am, then not, and now I am again. Oh, because I dared cross Queen Rhea? Aired her dirty laundry?" He cringed. "I wasn't even going for the pun, I swear. I apologize for that mental image which will haunt us all. But everybody's turning on me now because of... Remind me why? Oh, right, I did it for material for my book, right? Everybody's mad that I'm a writer and nobody's seen in my notebooks. Then, no, I did it because I'm mad at Shannon. Right? I'm—"

Rhea waved her hand in Byron's face, shushing, and said to Darius, "What do you know?"

Darius found himself unable to look at Byron's face, so he just responded to Rhea directly. "That poem that Byron posted on Facebook a month or so ago?"

Byron said, "What?! You must be—"

"*Shh,*" Rhea hissed. "Let Darius *talk.*"

"Shannon was having her shiftie at seat one," Darius recalled, "scrolling her phone. Byron came up to cash out. He was at the service end of the bar of course, right there next to Shannon, but she was facing in to the bar, and mostly just looking at her phone anyway, and she didn't see him there beside her. All of a sudden she started laughing and pulled up something on her phone to show me. She was on Facebook and had just pulled up the link to Byron's poem."

Chef Oz shouted, "I *told* you guys it was Byron! So, I had the right guy for the wrong reason, but I *told* you—"

"Shut up, Cosimo," Rhea said, "and let Darius finish."

Darius continued, "Shannon started reading the poem out loud and making fun of it. She didn't know Byron was right there, of course. She was reading it to me, sort of, but mostly just entertaining herself. The point is she had no idea Byron was listening as she mocked the whole thing. Like, brutally. I could see his face." He turned to Byron. "Sorry, man. I could see your face."

Byron sputtered, "But I didn't . . . You don't . . ."

Darius put his hands up defensively. "I'm just telling you what I heard and saw."

Rhea said to Darius, "So, you're saying you witnessed this the day Byron posted it on Facebook?"

Darius nodded.

Rhea waved the printed-out reviews in her hand. "I bet you if we look back at these Yelp reviews, the slew of bad ones all having to do with salads or desserts, cross-reference dates, I bet you're gonna find they started cropping up right around the time he posted the link to the poem. Day after, if I had to guess." She turned to Byron. "Eh?"

Byron's face was suddenly so pale that it was impossible for Darius to imagine he was wrong about what he'd heard and seen and hypothesized.

Chef Oz announced again, victoriously: "I told you guys!"

Orsa said, "Byron? Really? Over a *poem*?" She stared at Byron, then looked away, head cocked. "But hold up and wait. This still doesn't explain why he put a steak down the disposal. Why would anyone other than Shannon do something so petty and gross?"

Rhea said, "Because he knew it would strike you as something only Shannon would do."

Kenzie said, "And the steak went down the disposal shortly before staff meeting, so not long after you"—she pointed at Orsa—"sat down with the servers and told us who you suspected. Byron put the steak down the dishwasher after learning who you had on your short list, which included Julia, to make sure Shannon went to the top of it!"

Orsa said, "But this still doesn't explain where the steaks are. They did not leave with Byron on Saturday, he didn't have any way to transport them, they didn't all twenty-two go down the disposal, and I'm telling you, *on my life*, they are not in this restaurant."

It was quiet for a little bit, and Darius's thoughts snagged on this conundrum. Had he been wrong about the poem? The memory had stuck with Darius because although he was not a fan of Byron—whom he had observed romance and reject several nice young ladies in his time at the restaurant—he actually felt bad for the guy about the poem thing, watching as Shannon chortled away with her mockery. To be fair to Shannon, Darius had already read the poem before the shift, when the link first appeared on Facebook, and found it pretentious and obscure. Still, Darius had a heart; he didn't enjoy seeing anyone suffer real shame.

To this same point, months earlier when Byron's mother had come to the bar with a friend and spoken of Byron's use of his childhood bedroom as his writing studio, Darius couldn't resist telling Rhea later that evening. But pretty much as soon as the gossip left Darius's lips, he regretted it and asked Rhea not to say anything to anyone else about it. Byron was clearly harboring insecurities and there were people on staff—namely Chef Oz—who would ridicule him mercilessly over such a thing. Rhea agreed that they must not disclose this information to others, to spare Byron.

But this business with Shannon was another story. Because if Byron had in fact taken this route of vengeance, jeopardizing Shannon's job over a bit of teasing, then Darius didn't believe Byron deserved any protection. Not to mention, Byron's threat that forced the exposure of Rhea's socks secret—not that it seemed like Rhea planned to lose any sleep over it—was no small betrayal.

And yet there remained the issue of the missing steaks. If it was Byron and he was, as Orsa was convinced, incapable of transporting them out of the restaurant, what ingenious hiding place within the restaurant had he found?

Julia's voice rose from the corner of the kitchen where she stood. "It might be worth checking the dumpster," she said, tucking a stray hair behind her ear, "if it hasn't been emptied since Saturday."

Everyone turned to look at her.

Byron made a small sound, something like a dry, squeezed, gasp of a laugh.

"Just an idea," Julia said.

Orsa said, "The dumpster gets emptied on Mondays. Saturday's trash is long gone."

Rhea gazed at Julia. "But why would you suggest that?"

Julia tipped her head awkwardly in Byron's direction.

Chef Oz looked back and forth between Julia and Byron and demanded, "Well? Well?"

Orsa said, "Somebody say something!"

Byron blinked a few times then snapped the polishing rag he held into a twist and smacked it down on the stainless-steel counter before him. "You guys suck," he said. "All of you."

Chef Oz said, "I told you he hates us." He looked at Julia. "Even you. Sorry."

Rhea said, "Jesus, Oz."

"Truth hurts," Chef Oz said. "I've always told you guys he thinks he's better than us and he's using us, and—"

Kenzie said, "What do you mean using?"

"For his *book*!" Chef Oz shook his fists. "While the rest of us are busting our asses to serve food, do our actual *jobs*, he's hiding in the corner, taking his little notes, passing his little judgments, drawing his little assumptions, making up his little stories, always spying, sneaking, stealing... So it's just..." Chef Oz paused to kiss the tips of his fingers. "The guy who's been stealing from us all along finally got caught in the act. It's—"

"Your personal vendettas are all fine and good," Rhea said. "But the matter at hand, Oz. *We need proof.* About the dumpster, what Julia was about to—"

Byron broke in, completely ignoring Rhea in order to respond smugly to Chef Oz with one word: "*Jealous.*"

"Jealous?!" Chef Oz howled. "Jealous of a sad little man whose ego is so fragile some gentle teasing about—what was it? Some poem you wrote or something?—made you wage World War Three on this restaurant?"

Byron said matter-of-factly, "Jealous that nobody knows how my life will look five years from now. And everybody knows exactly how yours will look. Five years? Twenty-five years? You're a lifer, bro." He raised a shoulder. "No offense to any of the rest of you who plan to be here in twenty-five years, still taking orders from Oz when he's in diapers. No judgment. Just saying."

Rhea exploded, "Like there's something *wrong* with this work? Maybe some of us would rather do this—or *anything* honest—rather than whatever the hell it is you do!"

Orsa broke in: "But is it true?" Pointedly to Byron, she repeated, "Is it true? All of it. About the steaks. The book. What was the other thing? The poem. Shannon. Is it all like Oz said?"

"Well." Byron's eyes narrowed. "Seems like you all have your minds made up about me already, so what does it matter?" He swept his arm across the room. "You all think you know everything there is to know about me? Got it all figured out?" He pushed air through his lips. "And you accuse *me* of making up stories."

Orsa said wearily, "But is it true?"

Byron said, "Like I said, what does the truth matter if you're enjoying the story—"

"No, excuse me," Orsa said, twirling a finger in the air. "You're talking in circles now."

Chef Oz shouted, "*Of course* it's true!"

Orsa said, "How can we be sure? Who's got the proof? Where are those damn steaks?"

Shannon spoke forcefully, "Julia was *just about to say*, about the dumpster, if you'll all just listen, she was about to—"

"You know what?" Byron cut in again. "You all just feel free to carry on with your little investigation; don't let me get in the way. Keep telling your little tales about me. I'm gonna go have a smoke then finish resetting the patio. You'll know where to find me if you care to continue this absurd inquisition."

Rhea said, "Christ's sakes, Byron, don't start acting like some kind of martyr now."

"You coward," Shannon said, voice shaking with barely restrained anger. "I've been standing here, accused, listening to everybody air their suspicions about me the whole damn day, and you're gonna dip, go have your smoke right here in the middle of things because—"

"Yep, I am," Byron said. "Waste of my time. You'll know where to find me." He did a strange little curtsy then made his way over to the basement stairway and disappeared down it.

Chef Oz called after him, "Run from the truth, coward!"

Everyone looked around the room waiting for Rhea to ask again, and finally, she did. To Julia she said, "Why did you suggest the dumpster?"

"Well . . ." Julia released a few nervous, gusty exhalations. "Byron does this thing at the end of the shift, when trash is on his closing side work. Instead of taking the trash from the server stations and bathrooms out to the dumpster in its own bag like the servers are supposed to, you know, hauling it out himself," Julia explained, "he collects it in multiple bags and sneaks it in to either that"—she nodded at the large trash bin next to the dishwasher—"or that." She nodded at the other trash bin that lived at the end of the line, shared by Glen and Shannon. "So somebody else actually ends up having to take it out."

Wide-eyed, Rhea said, "What?! Back of house is already hauling five times more trash than us! *How dare he.*"

Gawking, Chef Oz addressed Julia. "Why would he tell you that?"

"I think," Julia said, "that he thinks it's funny."

Shannon said, "And I didn't think I could hate him more."

Rhea tapped her lip. "You're right, Julia. It definitely stands to reason that because he's gotten away with stuffing extra trash into their bins as part of his normal closing side work routine, that's where he would have put the steaks on Saturday night. Knowing they'd get hauled off for good on Monday."

Chef Oz clarified, "The evidence, gone forever, out with the trash."

Julia was nodding. "Not to mention, if the steaks *had been* found there, if by chance the theft was discovered before Monday and someone thought to look in the dumpster, obviously they would assume that a back-of-houser had done it, the steaks showing up among their trash and all."

"Smuggled them out with the kitchen trash," Chef Oz marveled. "Pretty clever actually, for a rat."

Darius looked around the room, clockwise from Chef Oz. Next to him, Glen was staring at the stack of empty plates warming under the lights before him. As far as Darius could tell, he had barely looked up from those plates for the entire confrontation. Next to Glen, at the far end of the island, Shannon stood with her berry-stained hands hooked over her hips. Her breath came in short and loud. Beside her, at the polishing station, Kenzie and Julia were both flushed, eyes darting. Near the coffee station to the right of them, Rhea was shaking her head, her make-up after this long day streaked and grainy under the harsh light. Orsa was nearest Darius, and her mouth snapped noiselessly open and shut again a few times, like a nutcracker.

Chef Oz demanded, "What happens next?"

Orsa's jaw stopped moving but when she did not offer a quick answer, Rhea piped up, "I'm off the clock, and"—she looked at Orsa—"I know I'm not exactly in your good graces right now, but if you want my managerial opinion, I'd say, everyone go about your side work like normal. Everybody's eager to get out of here after a day like today. So help each other out and try to knock things out nice and quick. Go about your work and let Byron go about his. Beyond that . . ." She looked at Orsa. "It's really up to you."

Orsa nodded. "I'm gonna go to my office and have Larry talk me through my legal options."

Chef Oz said, "I certainly hope you let me be there

when Byron gets canned. Or cuffed." He was quiet for a second, then added, "And I also hope you let me be there when you ask Lare about the legality of Rhea's little arrangement with the man in Mishawaka." He snickered.

Orsa shook out her head. "My dear husband would be so scandalized . . ."

"Trust me," said Chef Oz. "We all are."

Rhea rolled her eyes at Chef Oz. To Orsa she said, "I've already looked into the legality. There are no issues. No need to scandalize Larry unless you want to."

Shannon had moved from her station and now stood at the single window in the kitchen, located over the dish pit, overlooking the parking lot. "The rat," she gasped, pointing out into the dark night. "Look, he didn't go for a smoke—he's running away!"

Rhea joined her at the window. "Sure enough."

There was a scuffling, Shannon bolting for the basement stairway as this provided the quickest exit.

Chef Oz said, "Shannon, don't!"

Rhea called, "You're not going to catch him!"

They listened to the banging of her steps down the stairs then the slamming of the heavy basement door.

"What will she do?" Orsa addressed the question to Chef Oz. "What happens if she catches him?"

Suddenly, Larry appeared at the other end of the kitchen, sashaying through the swinging door. "Everything okay in here?" he said.

Orsa turned to face him. "It was Byron," she said. "Stole the steaks."

"Really? Huh," said Larry. "I really thought . . . Never mind. Doesn't matter. So, Byron! The server? Why?"

Chef Oz said, "Either to frame Shannon because she made fun of a poem he wrote, or to stir up trouble to get some new material for his book."

Rhea added, "Or both."

Kenzie said, "I guess we'll find out when his book gets published."

There was some laughter.

Larry said, "So did you catch him red-handed? Get a confession?"

Chef Oz said, "Nah. He was smart enough to get the evidence out the door already. I think him running into the night like a fraidy-cat is as good a confirmation as we'll get. Unless Shannon catches up and forces a confession out of him."

Julia had moved to the window where she gazed out over the dark lot and said, "Now that you mention it, maybe someone should check on her. Well, her *and* him. In case she catches up."

Rhea said, "Not it."

Larry said, "Did anyone else read the poem?"

Ant appeared at the swinging door to poke only his head in, and he looked around. "Hey guys, sorry to interrupt, but somebody just walked into the bar."

Darius said, "What's his vibe?"

"Tall," said Ant.

"That's not saying a whole lot coming from you," Orsa pointed out.

Ant said, "Nicest shoes I've ever seen. Some kind of loafer."

Chef Oz said, "Didn't take you for a shoe guy, Ant."

"I'm not. That's how nice they are."

Darius said, "Well, I'm off then."

Darius was daunted by the prospect of having to generate small talk or serve up anything other than shifties to exhausted staff at this point. But it was time to get back to the bar anyway to knock out some side work so he could get out of here at a decent hour. Hopefully the stranger with the nicest loafers Ant had ever seen would at least have the decency to tip well and vacate promptly.

Back at the bar, Darius delivered ice water to the bar guest who was indeed a tall, handsome, and smartly dressed gentleman who was gazing up at the TV, where a muted baseball game aired.

Darius apologized for the wait. "Drama in the kitchen," he explained.

"No problem at all," the bar guest said. "Still serving food?"

Darius glanced at the clock. "Late-night menu now. A couple of apps and dessert. Want to see a menu?"

The bar guest nodded. "And a wine list?"

Darius delivered these and while he waited for the order, he fiddled a little bit with the Pabst Blue Ribbon tap, which was pouring extra foamy.

PBR was Byron's go-to for his shiftie.

Darius didn't regret saying what he'd said back in the kitchen, as it was the truth, but felt a little sad nevertheless at the reality that Byron was guilty, and gone for good.

Byron was the only staff member who tipped on every shiftie. It was the unspoken custom that staff did not tip on their free drink; they might toss a buck or two if they went on to order a cocktail that required some effort or something like that, but not on the freebie. Byron, however, always left a dollar on his PBR. It was a little strange—Byron didn't exactly come off like the giving type—but a dollar was a dollar.

Darius wondered now if Byron knew the secret superpower of bartenders—to see and hear everything—and if all those dollars were a down payment for the moment that Darius would have the opportunity to either say what he'd seen and heard, or not.

Because, indeed, Darius had seen and heard plenty. He'd seen the strenuousness of Byron's efforts over the years, with girls and otherwise. He'd seen both Byron's manipulations and his sincerity. A few months before, he'd seen the initial joy, despite Byron's efforts to contain it, at news that his poem would be published—Byron was having his shiftie when he got word via email. He called his mom on the spot. He put his hand over his mouth while he spoke to her so that none of his coworkers would see or hear how proud he was; how moved; how excited; how relieved. "It finally happened," he told his mother. "Yes; online. There will be a link, so you can share it with your friends . . . Yes . . ." He continued, ". . . It's the one about Dad."

THE PANTRY CHEF

SHANNON JUST BARELY MADE IT IN TIME TO catch Byron. He was already in his white Hyundai with the key in the ignition when Shannon slammed into the side of the car with a thump, panting, unable to slow herself after running full tilt.

Byron startled at the impact of her body. She heard the automatic locks engage.

She rapped on the driver's window. "Open up!"

Byron turned the key to start the car. "Get out of here, Shannon," he called, without looking at her, his voice muffled through the window. "Out of my way." She heard him put the car in Drive.

"Don't be a coward," Shannon yelled, pressing her whole body against the car, then even leaning her chest over the windshield to underscore her resolve. "If you won't face me you're gonna have to run me over. Then you'll be a thief *and* a murderer."

He cupped his hand over his ear. "Can't hear you!"

She hollered in at him, "The longer you refuse to talk to me, the more people are gonna show up out here with something to say to you, ya know."

Byron's shoulders slumped as he shifted to Park and lowered his window a few inches. "What do you want me to say?" he said, staring straight ahead.

Shannon thought. She hadn't even had time to consider this. An apology? Is that what most people would desire in this scenario? Shannon put exactly zero stock in *Sorry*s. Her ex, the daddy of her baby, was full of them, but that never changed any facts or any fallout.

She was still out of breath from the sprint and coughed. "Now's your chance to get it off your chest. Just me and you. I'm all ears."

Byron said, "You got what you wanted, didn't you? Think I haven't been through enough?"

"But you did it, right? Like Chef Oz said?"

"Shannon . . ." The muscles of Byron's jaw clenched. "I'm leaving, gone forever, so you all get to say whatever you want to say about me. Drag me through the mud. Believe what you want to. Isn't that enough?"

Shannon sniffed. "Just tell me what you did. Simple."

"Wouldn't you rather just go with the story you've already—"

"No!" Shannon barked. "You keep *twisting* things, see? Everything you say is a twisting of things. Has anybody ever told you that? It's impossible—"

Byron held a hand up. "Shannon . . ."

She insisted, "Just tell me what you did and say it simply. Straightly. The truth."

Byron rubbed his fingers down over his face. All of his swagger from the kitchen confrontation had dissolved.

Shannon leaned closer. "Be decent. Talk straight."

"Okay," Byron said. Finally, he faced her. His light eyes were watery. "I tried to get you fired because you hurt me."

Shannon blinked, surprised by some element of this even though the facts had already been laid bare.

He added, "Sometimes I just get fixated on a thing." He suddenly looked lost, and old in the drooping corners of his mouth. "It's a problem I have."

"Huh." Shannon considered his choice of words. "I can appreciate this problem. And . . . the poem. I don't even remember what I said about it. But I definitely didn't know you could hear me. Although, I can't promise I wouldn't have said the same things to your face. I probably would have. I don't know, man. I didn't like it." She paused. "Or I didn't understand it." She threw her curly ponytail back over her shoulder. "I guess I don't appreciate poetry," she added. "What was it even about?"

"It doesn't matter," Byron said.

"Are you really writing a book about all of us?"

"It's not about any of you," Byron said. "Not in your entirety anyway."

Shannon considered this. "Isn't just using the parts that interest you even worse? What's that say about all the stuff you *don't* use—everything else a person is?"

Byron frowned. "That's not the right way to think about it."

"Okay." Shannon swatted a bug on her arm. "What

exactly *are* you writing down in your little notebooks all the time?"

"Just my thoughts on things."

"Thoughts on things?" Shannon guffawed. "What for?"

"If I don't record my thoughts, who will? Even if they're not interesting or intelligent or important, they're mine and I don't want them to just be gone forever. Right? Sometimes I like to look at them later and think about them again."

Shannon gave him a crazy look. "I'm trying to understand what kind of a person would want to sit around thinking about what they've thought about. I'm sure there's a word for it."

"A writer?" Byron offered.

"I was thinking more like egomaniac. A *writer.* Spare me. You think John Grisham spends all day thinking about what he's thinking about?"

"No," Byron said. "I don't."

"What do you think he thinks about?"

"Who the hell knows," Byron said, sourly. "Probably how to spend all his money."

"So what's your book actually about if there's no mystery, just little bits of this person and that person? And some thoughts about some thoughts?"

Byron lifted a shoulder. "Just . . . life. Nothing dramatic. Just life."

"That doesn't sound like a book anybody's going to read."

"Probably not. Maybe my mom."

Brightening as a completely unrelated idea reached her, Shannon said, "Hey, can I have your tip-out from tonight?"

"What?"

"The pharma dinner," she said. "I assume you made what, like, two hundred bucks on that table? Two fifty? Can I have it?"

Byron made a face, then laughed a strange laugh that did not include a smile. "I don't think it's up to me what happens to that money, seeing as I'm walking out. And if you think I'm ever setting foot in this restaurant again, you're delusional."

"But you did earn the tip," Shannon pointed out. "Even though you're walking out, I think technically it's still yours, right? You could claim it if you wanted to."

"Maybe you're right." Byron glanced back in toward the restaurant. "Then sure. By all means. Tell Rhea I'm forfeiting tonight's tip-out to you. I'm giving you—and her—my word, or whatever, that I won't take you to small claims court over it. It's yours to keep. How's that?"

"Your word or whatever?" Shannon smirked.

Before Byron could respond, Shannon spun at the distant slam of the heavy basement door of the restaurant and observed: "Your girlfriend's on her way."

"Oh, for Christ's sakes," Byron muttered, "she's not my girlfriend. And I . . ." his voice fell off as he searched for Julia in his own rearview mirror. "You know what? I really don't want to do this," he said, squirming. "Please don't make me."

"Do what?" Shannon said. "Stay here and look somebody else in the eye? Fess up?"

Byron nodded. "I don't care if it makes me weak. I know what I am. I already told you what you wanted to hear. I'll even tell you I'm sorry if you want me to."

Shannon said, "I really don't. I don't care for that word

at all." She stared across the lot for a bit. The tree line was inky black against the sky, which was a thinner, gauzy charcoal. She stepped backward from Byron's car and knocked gently on the roof with her knuckles, indicating he was free to go.

Byron had not even put his window up the whole way before the headlights were on and the car was in motion.

Julia approached Shannon and stood at her side. Together they watched his taillights lurch out of the lot and disappear hazily into the night.

"The coward," Julia said. "What did he say?"

Shannon shivered. Though she had been sweating a minute before she was now freezing cold, each bead of sweat an icy little prick on her skin. "He said I could have his tip-out from tonight. He's not coming back, obviously."

"So he's offering you olive-branch money that probably isn't technically even his to give." Julia shook her head disgustedly. "But did he say he was sorry?"

"I don't remember," Shannon said. "I think so. Who cares?" It was quiet for a bit. She regarded Julia sideways. "Did *you* like his poem?"

"I gave it the benefit of the doubt."

"He didn't want to talk to you, just now. Scampered off because it was you that was coming out. I guess he's scared of you now."

Julia showed her teeth.

"Maybe the next poem will be about you," Shannon said.

It was quiet for a bit before Julia said, "I don't think there's any chance of that."

Shannon was surprised by the sadness of her tone.

"What, are you unhappy about that? Unhappy that it's over?"

"I'm just feeling a little sorry for myself."

"About what? Dodging a bullet?"

Julia said, "Because of how much I'm going to think about him. Much more than he'll think about me, I guarantee you that."

Shannon made a face. "Why do you want to keep thinking about him?"

"I don't," said Julia. "But I will."

"Huh," Shannon said. "I guess you do have a lot of free time on your hands there at the host stand."

The basement door of the restaurant slammed again, and they both watched as Orsa emerged unsteadily into the night, locating the two of them, waving, heading their way.

"Look at her," Shannon said. "I know I should be mad at how eager she was to assume it was me. And I am mad. But sometimes it's hard to stay mad at her because she's just so . . ."

"Stupid," Julia whispered. Shannon snickered.

When she reached them, Orsa said, "I'm glad to see you two making amends." She nodded out at the road. "He's long gone?"

Shannon nodded.

Orsa said, "Did he say anything about me?"

Shannon shook her head.

"It's too bad he took off so fast," Orsa said. "Because now that everything's out in the open and resolved, I'm feeling a little generous. On my way out here I even had the thought, maybe I wouldn't fire him. Just accept his apology. Let bygones."

"Is that right?" Shannon said dryly. "A courtesy I expect you'd extend to any of us."

Orsa said, "What did he say, anyway? Did he apologize? Did he confess?"

Shannon said, "He told me I can have his tip-out from the pharma dinner tonight."

"Really?"

Shannon nodded. "I asked, and he said yes, and that was it."

"Huh," Orsa said. "Just to play devil's advocate, and I'm not trying to be a Scrooge about this, but I imagine his tip-out's probably, what, a couple hundred? Which is basically what I lost in the cost of the stolen steaks. So I think technically if anyone is entitled to Byron's tip-out it's probably the victim of his theft. If we're being logical."

Shannon stared at her. "I hope to God you're joking."

Orsa said, "I can see you feel strongly. So, you know what? Forget I said anything. Take that money. It's fine with me as long as Rhea okays it; she's the expert on that sort of stuff." She straightened the hem of her shirt. "That's pretty funny, though."

"What's funny?"

"That after a day like today, of all the things you could be thinking about, or worried about, the only thing you're actually concerned with is what's going to happen to—"

"It's *two hundred* dollars," Shannon said.

"Exactly," Orsa said. "Well, anyway, I'm happy for you to have it." She looked at her watch. "What a day."

It was quiet for a bit. The night air was alive with bugs and an icy breeze.

Shannon fidgeted, pulled the collar of her shirt away from her chest and peered down into it.

"What are you doing?" Orsa said.

"My boobs are about to burst. I was supposed to pump hours ago."

"You pump here?" Orsa asked. "Ick. That can't be very pleasant, in the employee bathroom. I don't understand the smell in there."

"It's not," Shannon said. "Especially when I'm all engorged like I am now. And when I'm wound up, it's hard to get to the letdown no matter how full I am."

"What's that?" Orsa asked.

"Letdown? It's when the milk comes out easily, on its own. Everything just drops and flows. Sometimes it happens right away, sometimes it takes forever. Being stressed makes it harder, waiting too long in between makes it harder, or not waiting long enough... And it's always harder when you're pumping versus actually nursing the baby. Anyway. Doesn't matter." She waved her hand dismissively. "You guys don't care about this."

Julia said, "I'm done with all my side work and the dining room is empty, I was about to clock out. Why don't you let me take over for you, finish up your station, and do your closing side work? Glen will be on bar food in case there are any orders since he's kitchen closer, right? I'll make sure when Darius does Byron's cash-out that he holds it in the drawer for you to get tomorrow. Let me just take over your station so you can get home."

Shannon looked at her. "Really? You don't have a clue how to do any of my stuff."

"Your side work is all listed on that clipboard next to the freezer, right? I'll just ask Glen if I don't know how to do something." Julia turned to Orsa. "Is that alright with you?"

"I don't care who does it as long as it gets done," Orsa said. "Danny will let me know if it doesn't. Nothing gets by Danny."

Julia turned back to Shannon. "Don't worry about pumping here then. Head on home so you can nurse . . ." Her voice dropped and she looked away abruptly.

Shannon said in disbelief, "You don't know my baby's name."

When Julia didn't respond Shannon said, "You don't even know if my baby is a boy or a girl." When Julia did not deny this either, Shannon turned to Orsa. "Do you?"

Orsa burped. "I'm thinking . . . a girl?" She glanced up, dipping her chin hopefully.

"Correct," Shannon said. "Congratulations." She looked back and forth between them. She said, "Her name is Ariana. She cries every time I leave her."

It was quiet for a bit, a frigid autumn wind wrapped around them, then the sound of leaves shuffling in the row of maples that flanked the lot. Eventually Julia politely offered, "Ariana is such a pretty name. Is it a family name?"

Shannon howled. "Are you kidding? I don't want her to have a *clue* what she came from."

INSIDE, SHANNON WENT directly to her locker to retrieve her things then exited back through the basement, deciding she'd rather not bother with goodbyes tonight.

The tired old maroon Chevy Lumina that Shannon and her mother shared started up with its usual rasping reluctance. Shannon turned on the heat and rubbed her hands together.

She pressed Play on the CD player. "The vineyards around the town of Barbaresco comprise nearly half of Barbaresco wine production," the man with the British accent said. "Wines from this area tend to be light but aromatic. More tannic versions of Barbaresco can be found nearby, in the Neive region."

Shannon pressed Pause in order to practice her pronunciation of this word, which was one of so many that were new to her: "Neive. Neive. Neive," she said.

THE THIEF

by Julia Simon

THE MAN HAD NEVER DREAMED. HIS SLEEP and life were otherwise normal as far as he could tell. The condition didn't really bother him and occasionally provided good fodder for parties—it was an easy way to derail the person rattling on tediously about their own dream life. Others typically insisted that the man did dream—he surely must—he merely forgot all of them. The man thought not; he thought, *I should think I know my own mind.* But it was never worth arguing about.

A girlfriend who dreamed prolifically became determined to facilitate the man's first dream, and she made no secret of the fact that she hoped she would be its star. She brewed him special teas and drew him special baths and did hypnosis before bed. She whispered her name in his ear all night long. None of this resulted in a dream, but the man began to find these and other aspects of her annoying, such as her opinions on matters of culture.

After this girlfriend, he was with another who accused him of lying about the dream thing for attention.

Then he was with another who said that she too almost never dreamed. They got along quite well, but this too ran its course.

One evening at a party, a woman mentioned that Welsh rarebit was believed to produce particularly intense and memorable dreams. In fact, she said, a group of writers in the early twentieth century had gotten together to eat the dish before bed, in the morning they all recorded their dreams, and this collection of stories was published. The man entertained the conversation because the woman was attractive, and he pretended he knew what Welsh rarebit was. The following day, he researched to find out.

He purchased the necessary ingredients and prepared it for himself that evening. He held no great hope of dreaming but it sounded tasty in any case, so he thought he would satisfy a curiosity.

After eating, he went promptly to bed.

In the night, the man was visited by the same individuals who always populated his dreams: the gray horse, the man who moved like his legs were boneless, his childhood cat, Dandy, the masked soldier, the clothed monkey, the baby, the woman with a red ponytail that reached the ground, the Ronald Reagan impersonator, the choir director, and the girlfriend who was so determined.

This group gathered just behind the man's skull and pounded against its interior all night, rowdy from the rarebit, chanting, "Remember this! Remember this!" The girlfriend's voice rose above the others: *"Remember me!"*

The man woke at the usual time the next morning. It had been a fine night's rest, but no dreams to speak of. Oh well, he thought. At least the ingredients he had purchased specifically for the rarebit—sharp Cheddar, Worcestershire sauce, and a pale ale—were perfectly good products that would not go to waste.

THE BAR GUEST

THE BARTENDER, HANDSOME WITH A GLEAMing bald head and neat black goatee, returned after a few minutes and asked the bar guest if he was ready to order.

"Glass of Sangiovese, please," the bar guest said, "and I'm leaning toward the brûlée. Would you recommend it?"

"It's my favorite dessert on the menu."

"Your late-night cook has a light touch with the torch?" The bar guest sipped from his water. "There are some online reviews about that, if you're not aware—scorched brûlées."

"It happens," the bartender said then hesitated before adding, "but you're in good hands tonight." He reached for a bottle of Sangiovese, uncorked the bottle, poured and delivered the glass.

The bar guest gave it a sniff and nodded with approval.

"About those online reviews," he said. "I gave them a look earlier tonight, out of curiosity. I'm in from out of town, wanted to read up on the local options. And it seems pretty obvious to me you've got a smear campaign on your hands. Even with some changes to spelling and attempts to disguise the voice of the negative reviews, there are aspects of the syntax . . . And so many of them, all scathing, all appearing in such a short time . . . Maybe your manager's already aware. I just thought I'd mention, in case not. I don't know if the restaurant has recourse. But management might want to consider the possibility of a disgruntled ex-employee, someone with an ax to grind."

The bartender wore a coy expression. "I'm not sure how much I'm at liberty to say. But I can tell you that you're onto something."

"There we go," the bar guest said genially. He raised and swirled his glass to admire the deep scarlet color of the wine.

The bartender said, "But like I said, if you're interested in a brûlée, our guy back there right now will make sure it's perfect. No burnt sugar from him. He takes it very seriously." A rack of clean glassware rested on the counter near the bartender. He grabbed a fresh cloth and one of the wineglasses, and began to polish.

"Dessert is serious business," the bar guest pointed out.

"Agreed. But our guy is as serious as they come. He's . . ." The bartender's expression changed. "He's a sad story, really."

"Oh?"

"I shouldn't say so. I shouldn't know what I know about him actually. Nobody should."

The bar guest settled back onto his barstool. "Now you've got my interest." He propped one of his feet up on his other knee and brushed the light suede of his loafer with his thumb.

Both of the bartender's hands were occupied with the polishing, but he did a stretch, back and forth at the waist. He held a goblet up to the light to examine for prints. "You said you're from out of town?"

The bar guest nodded.

"Then I don't know what the harm could be sharing with you," the bartender said. "Right? It's a sad story. God, it'll break your heart." He placed the polished glass on the mahogany shelving behind him and pulled another dripping glass from the rack. "You up for a sad story?"

"If it'll do you good to tell it."

"Right on." The bartender cozied closer. He gently blew a piece of lint off the side of the glass he polished and started in. "I went to grade school with Glen. Same class. Didn't know him well. He was a nice kid. Sorta shy, as I recall. Glen got lost in the woods near his house when he was maybe eight, nine years old. Dead of winter. Two days and nights he was gone. Finally, eventually, he found his way into someone's backyard. The family who lived there got him help just in time. He spent a while in the hospital and survived, but with some mental problems. Fell behind in class and ended up several years behind me because he kept repeating grades. When I got the job here it was the first I'd laid eyes on him since I was a teenager. I was surprised—relieved—to see he'd landed on his feet. But it startled me, seeing his face, hearing his name. Took me back. Made me remember . . . But he didn't seem to remember me. Or if he did, it seemed like maybe he didn't *want* to. I thought about identifying myself but then decided not to. Figured maybe he'd rather not have any reminder of the past."

"But he survived," the bar guest pointed out. "Rather miraculously, sounds like. For a sad story, it could've had a much worse ending, right?"

"Well, I didn't quite get to the crux of the story," the bartender said. "Although I did get to the ending, and you do have all the facts. So you can probably put it together."

The bar guest was quiet for a bit, considering. He sipped his wine. "You said he went missing and turned up in somebody's backyard, not far from his own home, two days later," he confirmed. "Meaning, no search parties."

"That's correct."

"And no missing person report," the bar guest ventured.

The bartender nodded. "Eventually just found his own way."

"Because no one was looking for him."

The bartender nodded. "Makes you wonder, doesn't it?"

"Wonder? I'll say." The bar guest shook his head sadly and wiped his lips with his napkin. "So what about . . ."

"His mother got a misdemeanor charge," the bartender said. "Neglect. That was the end of it."

The bar guest exhaled a low whistle.

"Like I said," the bartender added, "nobody's got any business knowing any of this. But, small town. People talk. The family that found him. The EMTs that responded. The neighbors. The story made its way around school. You don't quite know what to do with a story like that when you're a kid. You don't quite know what to say to a boy who . . ."

The bartender's voice shrank. "... with a mom who..." He gave his polishing rag a violent snap against his thigh. "Anyhow, nobody knew what to say. I still don't."

"Well." The bar guest shook his head. "That *is* quite a story. Does everyone here know it? Small town, like you said."

"They may or they may not. Most of the staff is a lot younger than Glen and me. The story might have no longer been the same story by the time they heard it, if they heard it. Or the little boy involved might not have had a name. Or they might have assumed it couldn't possibly be true. In any case, I've never heard anyone else here talk about it." The bartender scratched his goatee. "I've always assumed if anyone else here knows, like me, they don't know what to say."

The bar guest said, "Probably so. I wouldn't."

"The sad, true story of Glen," the bartender declared. "I told you it'd break your heart. My girlfriend was in tears when I told her."

"I imagine so," the bar guest said. He gently pushed the dessert menu back across the bar. "I'll take a brûlée to go with that sad story then."

The bartender reached for the menu, straightened up, did another stretch of his back. "I'm sorry to unload on you, man. I'm not usually like this. I'm hardly even thinking straight. It's been a hell of a day." He wiped his brow into his shoulder. "Bunch of steaks went missing first thing this morning, but even before that everybody was on edge because we were supposed to serve some famous writer who's in town for the evening, and—" The bartender suddenly stopped, took a step back, and regarded the bar guest. "You didn't mention what brought you into town. I don't read much fiction, so I wouldn't necessarily . . ." He squinted.

The bar guest looked away, shifting his cocktail napkin around on the bar.

"Never mind," the bartender said. He turned to enter the order onto his screen. "It'll just be a few minutes on the brûlée. Another glass of wine?"

"Not for now, thank you."

The bartender completed his polishing. He picked up the dripping plastic rack and headed out of the bar, presumably to return it to the kitchen.

The bar guest gazed up and down the bar. Candles in brass votives glittered over the marbled bar top. Some ugly art hung on the far wall. He was the only one in the place. After a full day of engagements, it was a relief to be by himself—conversation with a stranger in a bar could go any kind of way.

Just a few nights before, at a different bar in a different town for similar work engagements, the bar guest had found himself seated next to an elderly man drinking gin, who promptly launched into the story of his own life. The story the old man told was mundane yet amazing. It was so sad yet so triumphant, so full of joy and pain, so convoluted and so self-congratulatory, that it could not possibly have been the truth. The old man trailed off at a certain point, looking lost, and murmured after swallowing some gin, *Where was I?* The bar guest politely excused himself before the old man had found his way back.

The bar guest thought now about the old man and his life story then about the story he'd just been told. He wondered what version of his own survival story the kitchen closer told himself nowadays, and what version of it the kitchen closer's mother told herself. He even wondered, briefly, if the story was true at all or simply a fabrication by the men of this small town, to make an impression on their girlfriends—to bring them to tears.

Because of course a story was never as simple as the bartender had presented it: "*The sad, true story of a man*," although if you heard as many stories as a bartender did, it might be tempting to believe that. The reality was that for starters, a story was never merely one thing, such as, for instance, *sad*. There was always something else to feel, even if it was fleeting or discordant or impossible to name. Furthermore, the story of *one man* was never about just one man. There was always at the very least, a mother or a father, a brother, an enemy, a lover, a god. And most importantly, the bar guest thought, regardless of who was telling it, how near or far they existed from the source, and how hard they worked to hew to the facts, a story—as every storyteller knew—was never true.

THE DISHWASHER

WITHIN A FEW MINUTES OF BYRON'S AND Shannon's departures, Kenzie reported to others in the kitchen, where she was polishing, that Byron had unfriended her and all the rest of them on Facebook.

To Julia who was dumping wilted greens and garnish from Shannon's cooler as part of her closing work, Kenzie said, "I wonder if he took down that photo he posted of you." She held up a glass to examine for prints under the light.

Chef Oz said, "Nah, that'll definitely be part of the permanent collection."

Kenzie said, "It *was* a really beautiful photo."

Julia spoke haltingly. "It was? Was it?"

"Are you kidding?" Kenzie said. "I would die to have a photo like that of me. Everything about it—the scenery, the lighting, your candid pose . . . it looked professional. It looked perfect. I showed it to my boyfriend and told him he needs to start taking that kind of shot." To Chef Oz she said, "You said you saw it, right? Tell her how pretty it was."

"I'll do no such thing," Chef Oz said. "I'm old enough to be her father, you know. Yours, too. That's why, when I scold you, it's out of love."

Rhea looked back and forth between Chef Oz and Kenzie. "Oh, you two are friends now?"

Kenzie said to Chef Oz, "Quit talking like that, you're gonna embarrass Julia. You're only a couple years older than Byron, right? You're not old enough to be our dad. Just old enough to be . . . like . . . our much older brother."

Chef Oz laughed.

Rhea said, "Maybe photography will be Byron's next career move." She was refilling tea bag canisters. "Small town, word will get around about the theft and he'll be blacklisted at all the restaurants. So if the writing thing doesn't pan out, maybe we'll be admiring his work in *Vogue*."

Kenzie said, "I can actually see that." To Julia she said, "Can you?"

Julia was quiet for a bit. "I think Byron is going to find a way to get exactly what he wants. If he has a great talent, that's it."

There was a bit more chitchat and speculation about Byron's future, but it petered out quickly. People were exhausted, made quick work of closing duties, and slammed shifties instead of lingering.

By nine fifteen, the only people left in the place were Darius and a bar guest, and Glen in the kitchen.

Glen was kitchen closer for the night, meaning he prepared late dessert orders from the bar and was responsible for all final kitchen cleanup. It was an undesirable role on any night. Tonight, without a dishwasher, it was a nightmare. It hadn't occurred to Glen until others had already left that as kitchen closer he was also going to be left with a pile of dishes to hand-wash, as well as the closing duties typically covered by the dishwasher. Not to mention that his left hand, all bandaged up, was about as useful as a shoe.

But dining room traffic had ended early enough that Glen had been able to knock out a fair amount of work while he awaited final bar orders and drank decaf.

For that matter, the chaos of the evening and the wealth of remaining side work had proven a welcome distraction from his heartache over Jade. It was probably for the best if things didn't slow down enough to permit his thoughts to wander in her direction.

When Darius hadn't sent a food order by nine thirty, Glen thought it must be the case that whoever was in the bar intended only to drink.

It was always risky to do certain tasks such as final wipe-down and trash run and cleaning of the coffee urn before ten o'clock, but it was tempting to jump the gun. Glen decided he'd give it another five minutes before making his way to the bar to see if the bar guest was still there and if so, get Darius's opinion on the likelihood of a dessert order.

Glen rubbed the wrist of his injured left hand. A familiar little panic knocked haphazardly around his mind like a bird in a cage.

Momentarily the ticket machine came to life, startling

him as it always did this time of night, with its jagged purr. It produced a ticket which Glen read aloud: "Brûlée."

Brûlées were his favorite dessert to plate. They were beautiful and compact, required no stove heat and produced no additional dishes. The only challenge was applying the right amount of flame so you didn't scorch the sugar as Shannon did far too often.

Glen reached into the dessert refrigerator and withdrew a single ramekin, set it on the brushed steel of the dessert counter, and was reaching into the drawer for the small butane blowtorch when Darius entered through the swinging door.

"On it," Glen said, assuming Darius was here to retrieve the dessert.

Darius said, "You're not gonna believe it."

"What?"

"The bar guest," Darius said. "I think it might be him. I'm not sure. But it's a strong maybe."

"Who?"

"John Grisham. He's been nursing a glass of Sangiovese for a while. Polite guy. Said he was just in town for the night, on business. We chatted a while. And all of a sudden, right when I was putting the order in, it occurred to me. The Southern accent, the expensive jacket . . . I double-checked just now on my way back here . . ." Darius held up the Google Image results on his phone to flash them briefly toward Glen then looked back down to take a closer examination.

Glen said, "How sure are you?"

Darius shook his bald head back and forth. "Fifty-fifty it's him." He scrolled through some more image results, zoomed in and out. "The bar guest is wearing reading glasses, which Grisham's not in any of these photos. So that makes it a little harder to tell. And . . ." Darius zoomed in on a photo. "The bar guest's haircut's a little different than in any of these pictures. But the shape of the hairline and hair color looks right. I couldn't say for sure. But probably we'd better assume . . ."

Glen felt a buzzing jolt of adrenaline, followed by a firm weight as the reality set in: If the man at the bar was John Grisham, then Glen was responsible for the only food that John Grisham would consume at Aunt Orsa's.

Darius said, "Do you think I should text Orsa? I don't want to ask the guy directly or call any attention. I gather he'd rather stay under the radar. At the same time, if it is him, she'll be livid if she finds out somehow that he was here and I didn't know, or that I had my suspicions and didn't try to reach her."

Glen said, "Do you think she would come back in if she thought he was here?"

"For sure. Although maybe she's already asleep—Larry practically had to carry her out of here."

Glen said, "I think she would be upset if you didn't reach out now, even without being certain. I don't want you to get in trouble."

"You're right." Darius banged out a text while Glen peered down to examine the cold brûlée in his hand.

It looked just right, glossy and firm, the perfect shade of creamy yellow. No lumps, no separation, no drips or smears on the ramekin's exterior.

Darius reached for the canister of sugar which was closer to him and slid it down the counter to Glen. Glen hated when anyone else did this sort of thing in the kitchen—the risk of an untimely spill was never worth the satisfaction of a well-executed slide or toss. But Darius was an expert at this kind of stuff, loads of practice on the bar.

Glen spread a dash of sugar over the surface of the brûlée, without measuring. He'd had enough experience to eyeball a teaspoon.

Darius said, "You need a hand, with your hand?"

Glen shook his head. He fired up the flame on the blowtorch and gave it a few seconds to reach full heat. Then he carefully aimed the flame and spun the ramekin slowly for even distribution of heat. The sugar bubbled, browned, and became aromatic. He turned off the blowtorch and held the ramekin under the light to examine.

Darius peered at it too. "Fit for a king."

Glen set it on a saucer. From the pastry refrigerator, he retrieved a carton of blueberries and one of red raspberries.

He sifted gently through both for the finest, roundest berries, ones that looked ripe and ready to burst, but would not leak juice onto either the brûlée or the saucer. He had no trouble identifying the perfect blueberries, but the raspberries were a hair over, mushy and beginning to break down. He frowned as he excavated farther into the carton.

Glen could see Darius glancing at his watch, growing impatient to run the dessert, but Glen wasn't going to rush.

Eventually, though, he did give up on the raspberries. "But it won't be right," he said, "without some red."

In Shannon's salad cooler, Glen remembered, there ought to be the strawberries that garnished the mesclun salad.

To Glen's relief, he found that Shannon's salad strawberries were perfectly ripe and deep red, so Glen selected three, rinsed them, then used a paring knife to artfully slice and splay them on the saucer beside the ramekin, the interior ombre of red to white on display.

He set Maybe John Grisham's finished dessert on the counter to examine.

"Perfect," Darius said. "You're a pro, Glennie." He picked it up and placed it on a serving tray.

Glen knew Darius was just saying so because he was in a hurry to get the thing dropped. But it *was* perfect, the best-looking brûlée Glen had ever sent out. He had no idea what sort of brûlées John Grisham would have eaten in his life. Probably some great ones, possibly even some Michelin-starred ones. But Glen knew he had prepared the best brûlée that John Grisham—or whoever was seated out there—could expect to get in this town.

The swinging door banged behind Darius, and Glen was alone in the kitchen, his whole body still vibrating with adrenaline, eyes dry and throbbing from stress and so many hours under fluorescent lights.

Glen's thoughts turned to Byron. The idea of sabotage, not just of a coworker, but of *all* his coworkers, the entire restaurant, was so bizarre to Glen that he felt his headache intensifying just trying to understand it. But it wasn't only Byron that Glen could not understand. Byron was the one who had been egregious, and with ulterior motives, but he was just an extreme version of the pervasive attitude. The real tragedy was that enjoyment of everyday service seemed to elude nearly everyone in the restaurant except for Glen. There was camaraderie in complaining, of course. And there were glimpses of pride and pleasure in the work. But for his coworkers that seemed rare whereas for Glen it was something to look forward to every day. *You just had to care!* he thought. Why was it so hard to make a person care? If you cared, then plating a perfect dessert for anyone, anytime—whether it was a brûlée for Maybe John Grisham or a vegan apple crisp for the girlfriend who was sure to leave you—offered immeasurable satisfaction.

In fact, Glen realized, it was almost like a miracle if you thought about it in a certain way—the fact that, in a world where words could mean anything and therefore nothing, there were other ways to say: *I've tried my hardest; I've done my best; I hope you will enjoy and perhaps even remember this small thing I have prepared for you.*

DARIUS RETURNED TO the kitchen fifteen minutes later with the empty dishes, spoon tinkling in the ramekin; all that remained on the saucer were the strawberry stems. But before Glen had a chance to ask what Maybe John Grisham thought of his brûlée, the door behind Darius swung open, and Orsa was there, wearing flared jeans and a pink hoodie, her makeup smeared. "Did I miss him?" she panted.

"Only just," Darius said, setting down the empty dishes. "Five minutes ago. Paid in cash and didn't need change, so I didn't have any warning, and I didn't ever get to confirm it was him since there was no card involved. Sorry."

"Dammit!" Orsa said. She looked back and forth between Darius and Glen. "Well, what'd he drink? What'd he eat? Where'd he sit? What'd he say?"

Darius said, "He sat at seat six. One glass of Sangiovese and a crème brûlée. Said everything was 'just what he was looking for.'"

Orsa said, "So not *perfect*, or *best he's ever had*."

"But what he was looking for," Darius repeated.

Orsa said, "We'll have to tell Jane tomorrow. The Amish. That John Grisham liked her brûlée. I think we can assume it was him. I think it's safe to assume."

"Is it?"

Orsa said, "We're going to go with it."

Darius said, "Okay."

Orsa took her cell phone out of her pocket and clicked her fingernails over the screen. "I just realized," she said, "Edgar never responded to my texts earlier. I must have sent him twenty. I wonder what on earth he's doing."

Darius said, "I don't think he ever responds off-hours, does he? Funny that you mentioned him, though . . . I forgot all about him—*them*—with the drama of the day . . ."

"What do you mean *them*? Who's them?" said Orsa.

"I'm not trying to start a rumor or anything," Darius said. "But I came in a little early for my shift today, wanted to prep heavy for Grisham, and when I pulled into the parking lot Edgar was just pulling out, and Jane was in his car with him. Looking like she didn't want to be seen."

Orsa's eyes widened. "In Edgar's car?! You don't think . . ."

Darius shook his head vehemently. "No, I don't think. I was just surprised."

Orsa's face cycled through some peculiar expressions. "It's none of my business," she said, then repeated that a few more times.

Glen offered, "Maybe she needed a ride home."

Orsa said, "I honestly have no idea how she gets anywhere, those people and their rules . . . But you don't honestly think . . ." She squeaked air around her mouth. "You think they're more likely to tell me their secrets if I ask nicely like a friend, or demand it as their boss?" She looked back and forth between Darius and Glen then said, "That was a joke, obviously." She sighed. "I know there's a world outside of my place that's none of my business. I don't need to know if Edgar's corrupting her . . . or they're in love . . . or best friends . . . or if her horse just broke its leg or whatever . . ." She was quiet for a bit, looking downcast. "I know you all have your own worlds."

"And I imagine you do too," Darius pointed out.

"Do I?" Orsa touched the corners of her eyes like there might be tears, then sniffed. "Anyway." She brightened. "What I was going to say, though, was that it was classy of you not to ask John Grisham if he was John Grisham. Sometimes celebrities just want to enjoy a meal—or a dessert—in peace. I bet he liked that. Maybe he'll thank us on Twitter. You're a class act, Darius." She stretched her arms out and took a step toward him.

Darius said, "Are we hugging?"

"Class act and so handsome, too. You know I'd leave Larry for you in a heartbeat." Before he could respond, she protested, "I'm joking, again—take a joke! Jesus, you boys."

Orsa gripped and pulled Darius in for an embrace, then Glen too. She smelled boozy and sweet. "Thank God I had the A-team in here tonight. Can you imagine if it'd been Shannon on that brûlée? You two really have it dialed in. I guess you've had a lot of practice, closing together. Been doing it quite a few years now, haven't you?"

Glen and Darius both nodded in agreement. Glen wouldn't elaborate, of course, and he knew Darius wouldn't either, to tell her just how far back they went.

GLEN HAD BEEN startled some years ago when a vaguely familiar face showed up as a new hire in the bar. It might have taken him awhile to figure out how he knew that face, but when Rhea introduced Darius, first name and last, Glen remembered right away that they had been childhood classmates. Not close friends or anything, but Glen had a positive opinion of him. Glen had of course lost track of Darius along with the rest of his classmates, due to repeating grades.

Standing before his former classmate now, though, as an adult at his workplace, Glen harbored a brief panic at the idea that if Darius recognized Glen, he would almost certainly remember him as the kid who had gotten lost, who had fallen behind. And then Glen's whole history, including the diagnosis of *damaged* would be laid bare to the whole staff.

Fully expecting Darius to reveal this upon Rhea's introduction, Glen braced himself and he observed a flicker of recognition from Darius, then an expression of pain, which was quickly replaced by a professional smile.

Glen was surprised and relieved when Darius shook his hand as though they were meeting for the first time, and he followed suit.

After this interaction, Glen puzzled over what he might have missed or misunderstood about the look that passed over Darius's face and determined the look must have been one of pity. Darius remembered everything about Glen, Glen thought, and had simply had the courtesy not to say so in mixed company.

But as Glen thought more, he was eventually struck

by the notion that maybe the look was not one of pity, or anything relating specifically to Glen at all. Perhaps, Glen thought, Darius recognized Glen but didn't want Glen to recognize *him*, lest he be forced to acknowledge or recall something painful from *his* own childhood.

Darius had always struck Glen as a kid who had a lot going for him, plenty of friends, dressed nicely, performed well in class . . . but you never knew, Glen thought. Darius's childhood could have included any number of harms unknown to his classmates. For instance, Glen recalled, Darius was one of only three or four Black kids in the entire school. That couldn't have been easy. The pain on Darius's face upon recalling the past could have been a reflection of that, Glen reasoned, or it could have been anything, or it could have been nothing. You never, ever knew, Glen thought, what parts of their own past a person might be trying to leave behind. Better not to force a person to look back.

So, throughout the years and the many closing shifts they had worked together, the teamwork and the trust, Glen and Darius had never once spoken of their shared past. And for all this time, Glen was never quite sure who was protecting who, and from what. He didn't imagine he ever would know.

DARIUS BRUSHED SOME of Orsa's pink-orange powdery blush from his upper arm and looked at the clock that hung above the dish pit, which read 9:58. He yawned. "I'm gonna go lock up then start working on drawer."

Once Darius was gone, Orsa turned to Glen. "I hear

you're quite good," she said. "That's what your coworkers told me all day. They speak highly of you."

"Do they?" Glen was surprised to hear that anyone was saying anything about him at all. He started warm water running at the sink and squirted Dawn into a sponge.

Orsa said, "You're just about done for the night, right?"

"Just about."

"What do you have left to do?"

"Not much. I'll just finish up these dishes and any more that Darius has in the bar and needs help with. Then take apart the coffee maker and wash the implements. Then check and refill paper products in here . . ." Glen stepped away from the sink to consult the dishwasher's list of closing side work. "Then trash, then wipe down all these surfaces. Then sweep, mop, tidy the dumpster area, empty that ashtray, then lockers and lights."

When he looked up from the clipboard he could see that she was staring into the distance with bleary eyes.

"Hey, while you're here," she said, "and I'm here. I had a thought earlier, with all this stuff, the online reviews, et cetera. I was thinking that I really need to update the way I do things around here. The way I run my business. The world is changing, you know."

Glen said, "Okay."

"I've got a couple things in mind. I'm going to hire someone to gussy up our website and Facebook page, start actually posting there, really ramp up our online presence. Tweet at John Grisham, ask if he liked his brûlée. See what I mean? That kind of stuff. The reason I bring this up with you now is because I want to move all of my files to electronic. Get rid of everything in my filing cabinet, move it to a hard drive. So, would you help me haul a box or two of paperwork out to my car now? I'm gonna have Larry tackle this project and I want him to get started on it right away, like tomorrow morning. You know, scanning every paper and saving it on the computer, organizing all that crap. It'll be great. It'll help take this restaurant to the next level, and it will give Larry something to do."

Glen clarified, "You want me to carry some stuff from your filing cabinet out to your car?"

"Maybe just one drawer, if you're up for it." Her eyes traveled to his bandaged hand. "Although, I forgot all about that. Never mind."

"It's fine," he said. "I can't even feel it."

Glen followed Orsa to her office, where she opened the bottom drawer of her filing cabinet then yanked it haphazardly off its track. It was less than two feet long but jammed full. "How about that?" she said. "It's a beast, I'll get half."

As soon as she got her fingers underneath it, though, it was clear she was in no position to shoulder even a few inches of it.

Glen hoisted it onto his shoulder then steadied it like a large serving tray.

"Oh," she said. "Well, I guess you got it."

She led him down the hall, through the foyer, out the front door. He needed a break before descending the ramp that led to the parking lot.

Outside, it was much colder than he expected. It took his breath away.

He gazed into the lot until he located her white BMW SUV, parked just a few spots down from his rusted-out brown Ford Aspire.

On the pavement at his feet, next to the drawer, there was a dried-out and shriveled worm, and reflexively Glen thought of his snakes. Had he sent them off to a similar—or worse—fate all those months ago? He thought of loss, of torture and neglect. He knew their pea brains could not possibly comprehend betrayal or remorse. Nevertheless, he worried about his snakes every single day. It was almost a decade they had spent together. They were not warm, but they were a constant. He always knew what to expect from them; he always knew what they expected from him. Was that love, or the opposite? Jade had made him so confused.

Earlier in the evening, Ant the busser had asked Glen, "Do you live alone?" Glen was distracted at the moment and didn't realize the question was related to his injury and follow-up care; nor did he even realize he was being asked *with whom* he lived, versus *in what manner.* He answered, without thinking, "Yes."

Orsa followed his eyes to the worm on the ground, said, "Yucky," and toed it out of their path.

She was quiet for a few seconds then said, "Take all the time you need."

"I'm ready," Glen said, and he hoisted the drawer back up onto his shoulder.

He followed her to her SUV. She commanded the trunk open with a button on her key and the panel raised with a slow and controlled *whir.*

Glen eased the drawer into the trunk and wiped his brow into his hairy forearm.

Orsa pressed a button to close the thing then stroked it fondly like a good pet when it clicked shut.

"Thanks a bunch," she said. She pushed hair away from

her face. "I really am sorry about your breakup. If it wasn't meant to be, trust me, you're better off. But I can see you're taking it hard. You look—"

"Something is wrong with me," Glen interrupted her.

She cocked her head and regarded him. "I don't follow."

"I can't feel my hand."

"What? Oh my God, Glen, do you think you sliced a nerve? You should be in the hospital! Why did you just agree to carry—"

"No, no, what happened today isn't serious. The injury's just a clumsy result of the actual problem."

"Which is . . ."

"This hand is numb." He held up the bandaged hand. "Used to just be a small spot that tingled sometimes but it's getting worse."

"So when you cut yourself this afternoon . . ."

"I didn't even feel it. I only quit chopping because Shannon was screaming and then I saw the blood."

"Well, *that's* not good," Orsa said. "Jesus. Can I?" She reached forward to take his bandaged hand in hers, she cupped it there and looked at it. "Do you have any other weird symptoms?" she said. "Numbness. Nausea. Dizziness. That sort of stuff."

"My headaches are getting worse. And I don't always feel . . ." Glen struggled. ". . . like myself. I don't know how else to put it."

Orsa's expression changed. "Does your mother know about all this? The numbness, et cetera? If you were my kid—not that you're a kid—I'd've dragged you kicking and screaming to the doctor myself if I had to. Have you told your mother?"

"Well, no. She's dead. Long time ago."

"Oh my," Orsa said. "Long time? Young, then. Sad, sad, sad. What'd she die of?"

"They said it was a combination of things."

Orsa made a face. "A *combination*? Thought I'd heard it all before."

Glen shrugged. "They said with everything going on inside her, it was a miracle she made it as long as she did."

"I see." Orsa was quiet for a bit. "Well, what do I know? Maybe that's not so uncommon at all. What do I know? She did a good job anyway, raising a nice boy like you. I mean, man. A nice man. I'd like to think I would've raised a nice man. Or woman. I'd like to think. We'll never know."

Glen cocked his head. "You don't have kids? I guess I just assumed."

"You don't think my office would be plastered with pics? You don't think my kids would be working for me, if I had any?"

"I guess I figured they were off to college, that you opened the restaurant when they left or something like that. I'm not very good at keeping up with personal life sort of stuff."

"I see," Orsa said. "As a matter of fact, I opened the restaurant when I abandoned all hope in that department."

"Children?"

Orsa nodded. "Ship's sailed. But still chafes me, if you can believe that, even at my age. I don't know why I'm talking to you about old news. I guess you don't ever get totally over some things. You know, you'd be surprised what brings it all up. For example, you look at a person like Shannon. Wasn't wanting, wasn't planning, wasn't trying . . . Whereas I . . . Anyway. I'm not saying Shannon's not a good mom. That's not what I'm saying at all." She was still clutching Glen's hand but staring off to the side now, far away, eyes unfocused, into the night. "I don't know why I'm talking to you about this. Probably because of the limoncello. I'm not blasted or anything, just had a few. You're a good listener. Some people don't have patience. I guess it doesn't help that I'm a bit of a broken record with certain topics. Every time I bring this stuff up with Larry, he says, *Life doesn't always bring to the table what we ordered.* He loves a good pun."

Glen said, "That is a good one."

"Well, in any case, about the headaches and the numb hand," Orsa said, straightening up and looking at Glen's face. "I don't know anything about any of that. But it does not sound good. I lost my sister to cancer earlier this year. You need to see a doctor."

"I know."

"What's stopping you?"

"I don't have enough money."

"Oh." Orsa let go of his hand. "Really?" She scratched her scalp. "I guess maybe it's time for a raise. Is it time for a raise?"

Glen said, "I think so."

"Okay." Orsa swatted at a bug. Then she said, "Whatever you make now, I'll add a buck fifty an hour. Don't tell anybody."

Glen hiccupped, and to his horror, he started to cry.

"Oh, God," Orsa said. "Please stop. Make it two. Two bucks an hour more than you're making now, effective tomorrow."

Glen nodded. "Thank you." He sniffed into the back of his hand and managed to stop crying long enough to bid her farewell.

He watched as she pulled out of the lot. She didn't use a turning signal, but stayed in the right lane and did not swerve.

Glen hoped she wouldn't get pulled over on the way home.

Glen had been to Orsa and Larry's home several times, for the staff Christmas parties. He wasn't much for this sort of social get-together, but attendance was mandatory. This past year, Glen had drawn Byron for Secret Santa. He thought long and hard about a gift for Byron before eventually recalling that Byron had once complained of crappy hardware on his crappy wine key, offering this as his excuse for a botched wine presentation. Glen did some research and landed on the Rosewood Prestige Corkscrew, developed by a French sommelier. It cost more than the recommended dollar limit for gifts but felt worth it, especially when the thing arrived in the mail and Glen set eyes on it for the first time. It came in a neat velvet box. The stainless steel gleamed, the wood finish was striking and smooth. Glen got it out just in order to test the implements, snapping them in and out of place—everything felt tight, sturdy, and springy. Glen hoped Byron would appreciate its beauty and utility the way Glen appreciated his knives. Byron thanked Glen politely that night but that was the end of it; he hadn't mentioned it since.

Glen figured no one thing ever meant the same to any two people.

Well, and to that point, for his own gift at that same

party Glen had received an envelope from Kenzie and was stunned to pull out a hundred-dollar bill—far more than they were supposed to spend; more, even, than he had spent on Byron. Glen was so touched he could hardly find his voice to thank her. She said, "I don't know you at all. But I figured, nobody's ever unhappy about a little cash."

Glen said, "But it's so much."

Kenzie said, "But it's nothing."

GLEN'S WEARY EYES swept across the empty lot before him. At the far end, the *R* in the butter-yellow Wells Fargo sign flickered with no discernible pattern. Actually, he realized to his surprise after a bit more observation, there *was* a pattern to the blinking, it was just a longer loop than you'd expect; you had to watch it a while to understand it.

Glen turned back to the road and watched Orsa's red taillights weave and bend and grow smaller in the black night like the unblinking eyes of a reptile in retreat.

Glen was so tired now that the world had begun to judder and fray all around him, and he was tipping toward a dream. His mind went on a vast and wild and senseless journey as he thought again of his snakes, then of his life and his death. He thought of the bigness and smallness of his world, the miracles and mysteries and certainties of his life, and the two dollars an hour more that he would make starting tomorrow. He thought of all the ways that two dollars an hour more would change his life, and all the ways that it wouldn't.

ACKNOWLEDGMENTS

Thank you Michelle Tessler for ten years of generosity, guidance, and goodness. Thank you Jack Shoemaker for seeing more in every book. Thank you, Jane Vandenburgh, for wisdom and light, and Megan Fishmann for boundless insight and energy. Thank you to the best team: Dan Smetanka, Yukiko Tominaga, Rachel Fershleiser, Nicole Caputo, Laura Berry, Dan López, Wah-Ming Chang, and Alyson Forbes.

Thank you to my parents for fostering my early love of mealtime, and to my children for teaching me new ways to enjoy it. Thank you to my husband for cooking beautiful meals for our family—what indescribable joy it is to eat and laugh with you every day. Thank you to my sister, brilliant baker and artist, for contributing extensive knowledge of back-of-house mechanics and all things brûlée, and for walking with me on every path. Lastly, thank you to the many, many people I have worked with at restaurants over the years for the staff meals and the shifties, the lessons and the laughs.

© Rachel Herr

REBECCA KAUFFMAN received her MFA in creative writing from New York University. She is the author of *Another Place You've Never Been*, which was long-listed for the Center for Fiction First Novel Prize, *The Gunners*, which received the Premio Tribùk dei Librai, *The House on Fripp Island*, *Chorus*, and, most recently, *I'll Come to You*. Originally from rural northeastern Ohio, Kauffman now lives in Virginia. Find out more at rebeccakauffman.net.